THE BEAST FROM THE DEPTHS

Melanie jerked away from Tom and rushed into the surf. Then she vanished.

"Melanie! Where are you?" Tom called, his heart racing.

As Tom scanned the surface of the ocean, a snaky orange tentacle covered with huge, pulsating suckers thrust up from the water. Tom dived—only to feel another massive tentacle close around his middle.

Tom fought to get back to the surface, but he could feel chunks of skin come loose as the suckers raked over him. Clawing frantically, he managed to pry himself free and shot to the surface.

He got a quick glimpse of Melanie hanging limp in one of the giant monster's other tentacles. The mutant beast was coiled around her and squeezing hard.

"Melanie, hang on!" Tom shouted. At that moment a tentacle shot back up and circled his body again. But when he looked into the monster's gaping mouth, his blood ran cold.

Savage six-inch-long fangs were about to slash him!

Books in the Tom Swift® Series

A Hardy Boys & Tom Swift Ultra Thriller

TIME BOMB

Available from ARCHWAY Paperbacks

THIS BOOK BELONGS TO:

TOM SWIFT 11

MUTANT BEACH

VICTOR APPLETON

AN ARCHWAY PAPERBACK
Published by POCKET BOOKS
New York   London   Toronto   Sydney   Tokyo   Singapore

AN ARCHWAY PAPERBACK *Original*

An Archway Paperback published by
POCKET BOOKS, a division of Simon & Schuster Inc.
1230 Avenue of the Americas, New York, NY 10020

Copyright © 1992 by Simon & Schuster Inc.

Produced by Byron Preiss Visual Publications, Inc.

ISBN: 0-671-75657-5

First Archway Paperback printing December 1992

10 9 8 7 6 5 4 3 2 1

TOM SWIFT, AN ARCHWAY PAPERBACK and colophon are registered trademarks of Simon & Schuster Inc.

Cover art by Romas Kukalis

Printed in the U.S.A.

IL 6+

MUTANT BEACH

1

WATCH IT!" RICK CANTWELL SHOUTED. THE twisting road's sharp curves were coming fast.

"Chill out, Rick," Tom Swift said, sneaking a glance at his best friend. The young inventor expertly guided his van along the narrow paved road leading toward the ocean from Swift Enterprises' main complex. The wind whipped through the open window and sent Tom's blond hair flying. "This new lab— there's never been anything in the world—"

"I won't live to see it if you don't watch the road," his friend interrupted.

Tom enjoyed the irritated expression on Rick's face. In a small way it was payback time for all the practical jokes Rick had played on him. Tom took another corner fast, pinning Rick hard against his seat.

"You're the one who's always griping about how slow I drive. The sooner we get to the new Hydro-Projects Wing, the quicker we can finish and get to the beach." Tom hardly looked at the road, his eyes flicking instead to the dashboard. Bristling with dials and digital displays, it was more like the cockpit of a Stealth fighter than that of a van.

"Snails usually move faster than you do, but there's a difference between crashing and feeling the need for speed," Rick said.

Tom was pleased that his friend's sense of humor had returned.

"The van's computer safety system is operating at max," Tom said, pointing to a green light. "We *can't* crash." To prove it, he went into a four-wheel drift around another turn and took his hands off the wheel. As if guided by an expert race driver, the van corrected the spin, came out safely on a straightaway, and accelerated.

Rick let out a long, slow breath. "I prefer driving with hands on the wheel, even if you say a computer can do it better."

"You know I'd never recklessly endanger our lives," Tom said. "I'm just in a hurry to get where we're going."

"What are you planning to show me? The ocean?" Rick said.

"Out there on the old lighthouse promontory. See that silvery reflection?"—Tom pointed—"Swift Enterprises opened a state-of-the-art marine research lab a couple of days ago. We've got a half dozen experiments running already." Tom was tossed back in his seat when the van lurched.

"The engine! It's stopped!" Rick cried. His gaze shot toward the spit of land looming ahead of them. It was a long way down to the water, he knew. "Power brakes and steering need a running engine to work properly."

Tom smiled broadly. "Listen. The engine's still purring like a kitten. The electric motor's just kicked in, that's all."

"But, Tom, you took the batteries out of the van. I helped you do it this morning." Rick blinked as Tom steered the van around a sharp corner and along a road parallel to the steep drop-off.

"When we got within a mile of the new Hydro-Projects Wing, the van switched to broadcast power from Dad's new wave-action generator." Tom pointed to the dash. "We can't crash, and we don't need any fossil fuel. We can go forever, as long as we're within range."

Despite Tom's assurances, Rick heaved a

sigh when the van slowed and came to a perfect stop in the new wing's parking lot. He jumped from the van and closed the door, then looked at the steel-and-glass building and whistled appreciatively.

"That's one neat-looking building, isn't it?" Tom asked, getting out of the van. A quick glance showed that the three-story structure covered more than a quarter acre on the wave-worn rocky finger pointing out to sea. Communications dish antennas on the flat roof were partially hidden by weather-monitoring anemometers and hydrometers. A twenty-yard-long, five-foot-wide paved winding path from the parking lot led across the promontory to broad white marble steps going up to the Hydro-Projects Wing's entrance.

"Wait till you see the inside. The old lighthouse was a hazard, so we tore it down and built my new lab over its foundations. And down there on the beach—see them?" Tom asked, pointing over a low retaining wall running beside the path. "Those square concrete chambers form Dad's wave-action generator. It doesn't rely on tidal action, as the older one did."

"So it doesn't matter if it's high tide or ebb?" asked Rick.

"Right," Tom replied. "These chambers use falling waves to compress air and turn a turbine. When the chambers fill with air again, that gives an added boost to the turbine."

Rick was skeptical. "Those chambers power the entire building? They don't look big enough."

"They're deceptive. Dad designed them to blend in with the landscape. We can get forty megawatts from them," Tom said proudly. "But the really new stuff is inside the Hydro-Projects Wing." He took the broad, low steps up to the building two at a time. Rick followed.

When they reached the door, a pleasant voice said, "Good afternoon. Who sang 'Atlantis'?"

"You've used a voice-recognition access program," Rick said with a grin. "The same as at your main lab."

Tom nodded. "Donovan," he answered.

"Enjoy your stay," the computerized voice replied politely as the door opened.

Tom and Rick entered the building's lobby in time to hear a soft chime sound inside.

"That sounds like your phone, Tom," Rick said. "Maybe it's Mandy," he said, referring to their friend Dan Coster's cousin. "She might be checking up on you."

"More likely it's business and not plea-sure," Tom replied. "If it is Mandy, she's not checking up on me. We're just friends, you know."

"Sure, Tom, whatever you say," Rick said with mock seriousness.

Tom hurried to a low desk in the lobby and picked up the telephone.

Rick craned his neck back, studying the tall ceiling with its spidery webs of special structural steel developed by Tom and his father. Then he looked out at the magnificent view of the Pacific. The sun was dipping in the west and casting rainbows wherever its light passed through the beveled transparent surface.

Rick decided to look around on his own and headed for a small door leading off the lobby. The door stood open, so he peered inside the darkened room. Eight-foot-tall free-standing fish tanks filled the room. Rick went in and tapped the glass of one to attract a school of small fish swimming inside. Then he let out a loud yelp.

Tom rushed into the room to find Rick backing away from the tank.

"Tom, there's a giant in that tank!" Rick gasped. "Its mouth is wide enough to swallow me whole!"

"That's only George," Tom said, laughing. "He won't hurt you. George is a striped bass, a common *Morone saxatilis*. Besides, he can't get out of the tank."

"I knew that," Rick said, regaining his composure. He rapped his knuckles against the thick glass. "What is this? A magnifying lens?"

"No, George really is as large as he appears. He weighs more than five hundred pounds and is more than six feet long."

"Tom, we've gone deep-sea fishing, but we never saw anything like this." Rick studied the immense fish suspiciously.

"Hey, it's no trick. George is part of my growth hormone experiment. Using recombinant DNA techniques, I've developed a way not only to grow huge fish but to do it fast."

"Why bother?" Rick moved closer but jumped back when two more giant bass almost as large as George swam past.

"To feed starving populations, that's why," Tom said. "We can end famine throughout the world if we can quickly raise edible fish in the oceans and hatcheries."

"That would be fantastic," Rick agreed. Then he frowned and asked, "But what would happen if a shark got a dose of your growth hormone?"

"Remember the movie *Jaws*?" Tom asked.

"Sure," Rick said. "That was one big great white."

"Well, think of Jaws as a baby; then imagine its mother." Tom had to laugh when Rick shuddered and stepped back from the tall aquarium tank.

"You might be able to feed millions, Tom," Rick said, "but be careful you don't end up as food for your little pets."

"Don't worry, Rick. That's why I have you," Tom joked.

"My mother didn't raise me to be fish food." Rick edged from the room and stopped in the doorway. "What else are you doing here?"

"As I said, the entire Hydro-Projects Wing is powered by Dad's wave generator. Besides my growth hormone experiment, we're working on developing bacteria that can eat ocean pollution." Tom led the way out of the tank room.

"Like the bacteria that devour oil spills?" Rick asked, referring to the bioengineered organisms that could be released to eat the oil from spills.

"The Chakrabarty bacteria were our inspiration. But the field is wide open, and we've taken the idea a lot further. I'm working on creating a variety of bacterium that will eat almost any commercial pollutant."

"What if the bacteria get out of hand?" Rick asked. "It's all right if they eat sludge, but I wouldn't want them eating everything else once their food is gone."

"As with the Chakrabarty bacteria, I'm

using genetic engineering to make pollution-specific organisms. When their food—one specific type of pollutant—is gone, they die."

"Sort of like me," Rick said.

"How's that?" Tom looked curiously at his friend as they arrived at the entrance to another room.

"I'd be sure to die if the world ran out of pizza."

Tom laughed. "In this lab is a completely different way of doing research. My recombinant DNA techniques—" Tom stopped and turned when the lobby door opened.

"Who can that be?" he asked. "All of the staff who are voice-coded have gone for the day."

"Maybe George has a fishy girlfriend stopping by to pick him up," Rick suggested. His grin broadened when he saw Tom's sister, Sandra, enter the lobby. She waved and hurried over to them.

"Hi, Sandra," Tom greeted her. "What are you doing out here?"

"I thought I'd come by to remind you about the party."

"At Laguna Pequeña beach," Tom said, nodding. "We haven't forgotten. I was just going to show Rick my—" Tom stopped when Rick shook his head, put his finger to his lips, and motioned behind Sandra's back.

"Tom's got everything set up over here," Rick said, steering Sandra toward the aquarium room.

"Oh?" Sandra let him usher her into the room. George suddenly swam by, and Sandra squealed.

Rick was disappointed. He had wanted to scare Sandra as he'd been frightened by the gigantic bass. But Sandra's squeal was one of recognition. She rushed to the tank and planted a big kiss on the glass.

"How are you, George?" she cooed. "I haven't seen you all week. You're really growing." She turned back, her blue eyes dancing. "See you guys later." With a wink in Tom's direction, she left.

"Sandra helped me with the experiment," Tom explained. "She—"

"She knew about George," Rick finished, shaking his head. "Oh, well, show me the rest of your new digs. We don't want to be late."

"A pleasure. As I was saying, this is—" Tom never finished. An alarm sounded, then died as suddenly as it had begun.

"Something's happened to the wave generator!" Tom cried out as the entire Hydro-Projects Wing was plunged into darkness and ominous silence. "The power's been cut off!"

2

WE HAVE TO GET THE GENERATOR BACK ON-line, and fast," Tom shouted. "The experimental tanks need constant power."

"Don't you have a backup generator?" Rick asked.

"We haven't got it working right yet. Come on. We have to get down to the beach and check the wave generator before the fish suffocate." Tom raced through the lobby for the main door.

"Isn't there enough air in the water?" Rick took off after his friend.

"Not for a fish like George. He's so big he uses more oxygen than is usually dissolved in water. I have to keep a constant supply bub-

11

bling or he'll suffocate. The aquarium aerators run off the generator, like everything else."

"Then let's go!" Rick cried.

Tom worried as he ran down the steep trail leading to the concrete blocks that housed his father's newest invention. This failure could mean his experiments would be lost unless power was restored quickly.

The rocky beach crunched under Tom's shoes as he ran to the small building beside the looming structures. He was out of breath when he opened the door and hurried into the control room.

"What is it?" Rick asked, entering a few seconds later.

Tom's eyes darted across the panel, taking in all the information.

"The alarm we heard was a signal that the water intake was blocked. The turbine started again, and the alarm turned itself off. But the generator went off a second time, and no power came back on."

"Can you fix it?" Rick crowded close behind Tom.

"I have to look in the water intake chamber. You stay here. If I clear the blockage, the light marked Power will blink on. Turn everything off by hitting this red button next to the indicator light."

"Why? Don't you want the generator working again?"

"Sure I do," Tom said grimly. "But I'll have to go into the chamber. The turbine blade might start turning and cut me to ribbons when I free it."

"Count on me, Tom," Rick said, his hand already poised over the cutoff button.

Tom ran outside. He stripped off his T-shirt and kicked off his shoes. It took only a few seconds longer to skin out of his jeans. Then Tom took a deep breath, held it, and dived into the inky black water.

Strong strokes brought Tom to the water intake. I can't see a thing, Tom realized. I'll have to feel my way along the concrete chambers and hope I find the damage fast! Concern ran through him when his fingers slid across empty space. The safety grate is gone—I'll have to dive all the way down into the chamber to see if something got in and clogged the water outlet.

Tom jerked back when something slimy slithered along his arm and touched his cheek. Don't panic, he told himself, but whatever had touched him vanished as mysteriously as it had come.

Tom felt his lungs beginning to burn. He kicked harder and descended into the deep chamber, hands groping for whatever had blocked the blade.

He found the titanium turbine blade, then a long, thick rod that was blocking it. Tom probed carefully, trying to figure out what the rod was. About an inch in circumference, it somehow didn't feel like metal.

Ceramic? Tom guessed. Had a worker left something in the chamber? That didn't seem right.

Tom let a few bubbles escape his lips as he started pulling on the jammed rod. His feet braced against the concrete wall, he pulled with all his might. The rod in the blade snapped—and the turbine started spinning!

Turbulence slammed Tom against the wall, then sucked him toward the deadly blades!

Then Tom heard the turbine whine die. Rick had cut off the equipment just in time.

Dazed, Tom dropped the rod, kicked weakly, and rose to the surface. He gulped in badly needed air and for several seconds floated on his back, letting the warm Pacific water splash his face. Then he swam back to the beach. By the time he got there, he had recovered.

"Tom, are you all right?" Rick asked anxiously.

"Fine, just fine," Tom said. "But that sure was a close call. Something tore off the safety grate and got jammed into the blades and clogged the drain." Then Tom remembered the jellyfish-like touch on his cheek and shivered.

Rick peered closely at his friend. "I can take you to a doctor—"

"Don't worry, Rick," Tom said. "Something slick and slimy touched me in the chamber, but it didn't hurt me. I wonder what was caught in the blades? It didn't feel like metal. More like . . ."

"What?" Rick asked. "What did it feel like?"

"Bone," Tom said. "Some very big fish must have gotten caught."

He shook water out of his eyes, then said to Rick, "I'm going to restart the turbine, which should clear the drain, then call out a maintenance crew to fix that grating. I don't think there'll be any more trouble before they get here."

"Good," Rick said. "I wouldn't want George going belly up. And we've got a party to get to!"

"The Scavengers are really hot tonight, aren't they?" Rick said between mouthfuls of hot dog.

Tom nodded. Dan Coster's band had never sounded better, and being out on Laguna

Pequeña beach let them crank up the volume. Most of the stores along the beach were closed for the evening, but those still open welcomed the late-night revelers. Tom was pleased to see how many people were there. He, Sandra, and their friends supported the Laguna Pequeña Merchants Association, which had been generous in sponsoring after-school dances, donating money for the new football scoreboard, and giving the students from Jefferson High a place to enjoy themselves.

"Hi, guys," Sandra Swift said. She pushed between Tom and Rick. "I want to dance. How about it, Rick? Can I drag you away from the food long enough?"

"For you, anything," Rick replied, but he looked longingly at a second hot dog on his plate. Then he shrugged and let Sandra lead him away to dance on the far side of the fire built in a pit in the sand. Rick and Sandra had dated for a while, and everyone knew that Rick was stuck on his best friend's sister.

Tom watched Rick and Sandra dancing and wished he could relax. He kept thinking of the new wave generator and what might have jammed the turbine. Tom reached into his pocket for his portable phone, then realized he had left it in his van. He wanted to call and get a progress report on the repair work.

He had just started for the parking lot when Dan Coster finished his song.

"We're taking a break," Dan was shouting into the mike. "The Scavengers will be back in ten minutes!"

Dan hopped down from the small stage and jogged over to Tom. "Hey, Tom-Tom, where are you off to? The dance is just getting going." Dan slapped Tom on the back.

"You and the band are doing great," Tom said.

"I just hope we're good enough," Dan said. "The band is going to get attention, no matter what."

"I thought you'd already signed a contract to play," Tom said. The Scavengers were the scheduled headlining group at the Laguna Pequeña Surfing Invitational, sponsored by the merchants association and Super-Glide Surfboards.

"Well, yes and no. The local cable television company is still negotiating for national pickup of the surfing competition. If they drum up enough interest, everybody will see us—and hear us. Super-Glide will definitely get on board for national coverage if enough money from Central Hills is pledged."

"And if the Scavengers don't get to play," Tom prompted his friend, "what happens then?"

"Why, I win the surfing competition walking away, and the band gets some press that way. But the invitational is going to be big, Tom-Tom, real national stuff. This is our break."

Tom looked up and down the beachfront. Since many of the surfing crowd had moved farther north to the bigger Playa Bonita beach, the stores had fallen on hard times. For them the invitational might mean the difference between going bankrupt and staying alive.

Just as Tom turned, a camera flash blinded him.

"Smile, Tom," Dan said. "Everybody wants my picture, and I ought to be surrounded by people who look as if they're enjoying themselves."

Tom blinked hard to clear his vision of the afterimage from the flash. "Dan," he said, "you weren't even facing that camera—I was."

"Well, maybe you've got a secret admirer," Dan said with a grin. "I saw a girl in the crowd scoping you out with her Nikon during the first set."

Tom shrugged off Dan's comment. His friend was always trying to goad him. There was no reason why people shouldn't be taking pictures at a beach party. Tom remembered the call he wanted to make. He turned to Dan and said, "Look, I've got to go."

"No way! The fun's just getting started. And there's Mandy. Hey, Mand—over here!" Dan waved to a girl making her way through the crowd.

Mandy Coster saw her cousin and Tom, smiled, and waved. Tom decided he could put off checking on the repair crew. Mandy's long chestnut hair was caught on a sea breeze and fluttered like a banner. She was wearing a white terry-cloth jacket over her red swimsuit and carried a large rolled-up beach towel.

"Sorry I'm so late," Mandy said as she approached Tom and Dan. "A friend from back east called, and it took forever to get her off the phone, and then I had to beg a ride down here from my mom."

"You're just in time," Dan said. "We're cranking up the volume for the second set, and I want to see you two out there dancing." Dan grinned and ran back to the small stage.

"It looked as if you were getting ready to leave, Tom. Have you been here long?" Mandy asked.

"Not too long. But Rick and I found a problem up at the new lab, and I wanted to call and check on it," Tom said, just as another flash caught him square in the face. Mandy turned to see who had taken the picture, but whoever it was had disappeared back into the crowd.

"Sandra was telling me about the new Hydro-Projects Wing. Is the problem too serious for you to give me a tour?" Mandy asked, dropping her towel on the sand.

"No, not really. We can—" Tom started to say. Then talking became impossible. Dan had kept his promise. The volume was up to the limit of human endurance, but no one seemed to mind.

Tom smiled. He took Mandy's hand, and led her toward the stage. They found a small space in the crush and began to dance. Tom found himself relaxing.

He and Mandy had gone out, off and on, for a while, and though they weren't dating steadily, Tom looked forward to the time he spent with her.

Ten minutes later, as the band was tuning up for its next number, Tom said, "I need something to drink. How about you?"

"I could use a soda," Mandy said. "I'll spread out the towel."

"I'll be right back," he promised. Tom dodged through the crowd to the large ice chests. He pawed through the ice until he found Mandy's favorite soda, then stopped when a flash went off in his face again.

He looked up and saw a tall, thin, dark-haired girl about his age. She was peering through her camera's viewfinder to take his picture. When she saw that Tom had noticed her, she snapped another picture, then turned and hurried off.

"Wait!" Tom cried, dropping the can of soda and running after her. He wanted to know if she was the one who had been taking his picture all evening.

The girl stayed ahead of him. The waves lapped against the beach and washed away her footprints as she ran with long, graceful strides.

"Hey, stop! I just want to talk," Tom called. The girl looked back, as if considering this. Then she put on a burst of speed that momentarily left him behind.

Tom knew he could overtake her, but a scream from the party stopped him in his tracks. He looked at the dark figure of the girl and watched her vanish into the night.

Another, louder scream cut through the night air. It was a female voice, filled with sheer terror.

3

THE SCREAM STILL RINGING IN HIS EARS, TOM ran as fast as possible. When he got back to the party, everyone was standing at the edge of the water. A blond girl wearing a green one-piece swimsuit was in the center of the crowd, sobbing and pointing toward the surf.

"There!" she cried. "It happened out there!"

"What's going on?" Tom asked, stopping beside his friends.

Dan Coster answered. "We took a break and decided to go for a swim. Amber went out farther than the rest of us. She panicked, I guess."

"I did not!" the girl retorted, flaring up. "It

grabbed me. I was swimming and felt something touch my leg. Then it grabbed me!" Amber reached down to show where the mysterious attacker had grasped her leg, then screamed again when she saw a small wound there.

"Sit down over here by the light. Let me look at it," Tom said, guiding her toward the stage.

"Tom's good at fixing up minor cuts," Sandra said, putting her arm around Amber's shoulders. Her presence seemed to calm the near-hysterical girl.

Tom touched the wound and felt something hard embedded in Amber's skin.

"This might hurt a bit. Rick," Tom called, "go get the first-aid kit from my van." He caught the hard object between his fingers and pulled quickly, before Amber realized what he was doing. Only after he extracted the object did the wound begin to bleed.

"Don't worry, Amber," Mandy said soothingly. "We'll get you fixed up just fine."

"It's not serious," Tom said. Rick handed him the first-aid kit. Tom quickly dabbed hydrogen peroxide onto the puncture, then put a bandage over it. "There, all done. You might want to get a doctor to check it."

"I feel kind of dumb for yelling like that," Amber said, getting back her composure.

"The cut isn't that bad. I wouldn't have even noticed it except—" She glanced out into the surf and shivered.

"Let's just sit awhile," Sandra suggested. Amber agreed.

"She'll be okay, won't she, Tom?" Rick asked.

"I don't think the wound will get infected— we cleaned it up right away." Tom opened his hand and looked at the long, thin white object he had pulled from Amber's leg.

"What's that?" Dan asked. He took it from Tom and held it up.

Tom recognized it immediately. "A tooth," he said. "A piece of a huge fish tooth."

"What kind? It's three inches long," Dan said. He tossed it back to Tom, who caught it deftly.

"Maybe it's from George," Rick suggested. "It's about the right size."

Tom went cold inside. Rick was right about the size—the tooth could have come from the giant bass. But George was safe in his tank.

"Hey, everybody," Dan shouted, "let's not gloom and doom around. This is a party. Back into the water. Last one in is a jelly-fish!" Dan ran into the surf, caught a wave, and plunged into the dark water. He surfaced a few yards farther out and swam powerfully.

Tom looked from his friend out in the ocean

back to where Mandy and Sandra were sitting with Amber. He was uneasy about anyone going back into the water without knowing more about the fish that had bitten Amber Bradley. Opening his hand, he examined the tooth again in the flickering light from the campfire on the beach.

It was a fish tooth all right. But from what kind of fish?

"Let's go, Tom. Dan's right. We're here to have fun." Rick took off for the water and duplicated Dan's clean dive into the surf. The members of the Scavengers wasted no time joining in the revelry.

Tom took one last look at the giant tooth before slipping it into a small zippered pocket in his trunks. Then he went after the others, letting the warm ocean water close over him. He swam out a dozen yards, then treaded water.

"This is great, isn't it, Tom-Tom?" Dan called. He paddled out a bit farther.

"It's fun," Tom agreed, "but I'd like to find out what happened to Amber."

"Just a fluke. Like on a whale. Get it?" Dan laughed at his own joke.

Tom snorted and began swimming slowly through the waves. The water wasn't good for surfing that night, but it was perfect for a leisurely swim. Right after sunrise was always the best surfing at Laguna Pequeña.

"Tom, it's got me!" Dan suddenly shouted. "It's big and black and coming up from the bottom after me!"

Tom saw his friend's arms go straight up in the air an instant before Dan slipped under the surface. Tom kicked and stroked frantically to reach him.

Dan surfaced ten feet away, splashing and yelling. "It's after me. It's eating me alive!" Again he vanished under the waves.

By this time Rick was swimming to Dan's rescue. Tom waved to him. "Hold on, Rick. Wait for him to come up again."

"But, Tom," Rick protested, "Dan's in trouble. Even good swimmers can get into trouble."

Just then Dan surfaced closer to shore, laughing at them. "Boy, did you guys look dumb. You thought the beast from twenty thousand fathoms was chewing on me!"

Exasperated, Tom rolled onto his back and let the waves carry him up and down, the warm water breaking over him. The stars above were hard, clean points. Tom wanted to reach up and take one and give it to Mandy.

"Mandy!" he cried, thrashing around. He rolled over and bobbed up. Distracted by the mystery-girl photographer and Amber Bradley's being bitten, he had forgotten her.

Still, Rick's comment that the fish tooth might belong to George gnawed at Tom. He vowed to get back to the Hydro-Projects Wing and check his growth hormone experiments. Theoretically there wasn't any way one of his specimens could have escaped—but he wasn't certain. The wave generator shouldn't have jammed, either.

"Hey, Tom-Tom, where you going?" yelled Dan, floating lazily on the waves.

"To shore," Tom replied. "Too much has been happening, and I've been ignoring—" Tom cut off his words when he saw the moonlit waters around Dan Coster turn black as midnight just below the surface.

"Dan!" Tom shouted. "Swim for shore! Under you! It's coming up from the bottom!"

Dan laughed, dipped his face into the water, and took a mouthful. He spit the water out in a high fountain. "That's what I think of your joke, Tom. Didn't anyone ever tell you to think up your own gags?"

"Dan, swim!" Tom started toward his friend, wondering if the sounds of his approach would distract the hulking figure in the water. Sharks often attacked if a swimmer flailed around too much. As he pulled close to Dan with strong, clean strokes, Tom hoped this wasn't a shark. One bite and Dan would be history.

Tom went cold inside when he remembered what he had told Rick earlier about a shark's getting a dose of his growth hormone.

"Dan, swim!"

"Yeah, Dan, you've been loafing about. I'll race you to the beach," called the band's bass guitar player as he began swimming with more energy than skill to entice Dan to real competition.

Tom swam, watching the dark shape pace Dan. He waved to Rick, who was swimming closer to the beach with several girls. Rick saw the dark mass moving in the water and turned to warn the girls with him. They swam for the beach, heading away from the black mass. Only then did Rick join Tom.

"What *is* that thing?" Rick asked. "It's a monster."

"It might be what bit Amber," Tom said. Together they closed in on Dan, who had quit the race and let his friend go ashore alone. He was rolling over and over in the water—right in the black shape's path!

Tom and Rick swam as hard as they could. Tom came up on Dan's right side and Rick on his left. Dan protested as they pushed him toward the beach. Only then did he see the danger.

"Yipes!" Dan cried. He shot forward, Tom and Rick on either side. But the shape rose under them, lifted them, and tossed them aside as if they were nothing more than annoying drops of water.

They surfaced, sputtering, and watched as the hulk surged past them toward the beach. Tom and the others were now close enough to shore to get their feet under them and scramble out of the water. The beach was in turmoil as the boisterous partygoers scattered before the monstrous shape that now rose out of the water like a breaching whale. It rose impossibly high, blocking out the moon before it crashed back down, half of its huge body in the surf, the other half on the sand.

Tom rushed to join Mandy, Sandra, and Amber. Huddled together, they saw that the thing had stopped moving. The crowd remained frozen in stunned silence for a few seconds. Then everyone started talking and crowding around the hulking creature.

"What's going on?" came the loud question. "Get back from that. Don't you kids have any sense? Back—get away from it!" Two uniformed police officers were pushing through the crowd.

"Officer," Tom started, "we were swimming when—"

"Go home," the policeman said, cutting Tom off. "All of you."

The officer used a walkie-talkie to call in his report. The party was definitely over.

"Can I give you a lift?" Tom asked Mandy.

"I'll go with Dan, thank you," Mandy said in a cold voice.

"Okay," Tom said. He caught her mood and felt guilty, but he couldn't take his eyes off the mountainous fifty-foot-long-carcass on the beach. Once again Tom's own words came back at him: imagine that Jaws was a baby, and try to picture his mother.

Although it was a warm evening, cold sweat gave him a sudden chill. Tom raced from the beach to the parking lot, forgetting about Rick, Sandra, Mandy, and the mystery girl with the camera. He hopped into his van and moments later was on the highway, zooming toward the new Hydro-Projects Wing.

4

S**URF'S UP!**"

Tom Swift saw Dan Coster running toward the water. Twenty yards down Laguna Pequeña beach lay the cordoned-off carcass that Tom had been eyeing from a distance since sunrise. Tom had spent the night at the new wing looking for answers. His exhaustive efforts had assured him the strange beast was not the result of his own experiments with growth hormones. But it could have been, and that knowledge left Tom feeling uneasy. Unable to sleep, he had driven back to the beach to study the remains of the improbable monster.

"Hey, Tom, you going to sit there or are

you going to get wet?" Dan shoved his surf-board into the sand and sank down cross-legged next to Tom. "We're getting in some practice for the invitational."

Slowly Tom turned his attention to Dan. "Nobody's out today," Tom said. "The car-cass is keeping them away."

"All the more water for us. The police said we could surf if we didn't come ashore within twenty yards of it." Dan slapped Tom on the shoulder. "Come on, guy. Get a wet suit on and let's go. That monster's one of a kind and won't bother us anymore."

"I do have my stuff in the van," Tom said. He came to a quick decision. "Sure, why not?"

"Let's show 'em some fancy board work." Dan shot to his feet, grabbed his board, and dived into the surf, paddling hard.

Tom went to his van, pulled out his black-and-yellow-striped wet suit, and started to unzip it when an insistent beeping distracted him. He took his miniphone from his pocket and flipped it open. His father's face showed in the small TV screen set into the top.

"Yes, Dad, what is it?"

"Tom, can you come to the administration building immediately? It's about last night's incident at Laguna Pequeña."

"Be right there," Tom said. He saw Dan

catch the first wave and start in. Tom heaved a sigh. There wasn't time to test the surf, even for a single ride. He waved to Dan, gave a shrug and headshake by way of explanation, then got into the van and drove to the main complex of Swift Enterprises.

Tom sucked in his breath when he saw the cars in the parking lot outside the glass-faced building in the center of the Swift Enterprises complex. A police cruiser was parked next to a car bearing the plates of the mayor of Central Hills, Hector Zamora.

Tom hurried into the administration building, took an elevator to his father's top-floor office, and greeted Mary Ann Jennings, the receptionist.

"Good morning, Tom. Your father's expecting you," Mary Ann said. "Go on in."

Tom usually stopped to chat, but not now. He went into his father's office.

"Tom, glad you got here so fast. You know Mayor Zamora and Chief Montague." Mr. Swift motioned for Tom to be seated on a couch to one side of the office.

Tom knew and respected the Central Hills police chief, Robin Montague. He shook hands with her and the mayor. Hector Zamora's expression was a mixture of annoyance and concern. From the way he kept glancing at the third city official in the room, Tom knew why.

"You haven't met Mitch Carlton," Mr. Swift continued. "Mr. Carlton is director of the city health department."

"And an undeclared candidate for mayor," Tom added. He caught Mayor Zamora's expression and knew Carlton was the source of his irritation. The two had locked horns several times over public health concerns. Tom thrust out his hand to shake.

"Let's cut the chitchat, Mr. Swift," Mitch Carlton said, ignoring Tom completely. "We've got a major health problem on our hands, and I don't see how inviting your high school student son to join us will help solve anything."

"Tom's been doing some research that might have a bearing on the problem," Mr. Swift said, keeping his tone even.

"I doubt it," Carlton said testily. "We've got a dead marine animal that nobody in our department can positively identify stinking up Laguna Pequeña beach. Unless you tell me it's your son's pet, I doubt there's anything he can contribute."

Although Tom tried to make eye contact, Carlton never turned in his direction, addressing only Mr. Swift.

"I took this from a wound a girl got last

night while swimming," Tom cut in. "Do you think it belongs to the beached marine animal?" Tom held up the tooth he had removed from Amber's leg and handed it to the mayor.

Mitch Carlton snatched it out of Zamora's hand and held it up for closer examination. "This might be from the beast, but I doubt it."

"Why is it so hard to identify the creature?" asked Tom.

"We think it might be an orca," Carlton said, "but it has certain strange aspects to it."

"What happened last night, Tom?" Mr. Swift asked.

Tom gave a concise account of how Amber Bradley had been attacked and the way Dan Coster had seemingly been chased ashore by the marine creature.

"I don't think the beast was alive, though," Tom finished. "It was coming in on the tide rather than swimming under its own power."

"That agrees with my analysis," Carlton said. "The thing has been dead for some time."

"Mayor Zamora," Mr. Swift said, "we at Swift Enterprises want to help any way we can. If you'd permit Tom a closer look at the carcass, he might be able to give you a fresh insight."

"Why him?" Carlton demanded. "Some kid

who took one high school biology course isn't going to be much help."

"He'll have the full backing of Swift Enterprises. We have cutting-edge technology in marine research and a dozen different branches of biology." Mr. Swift directed his comments to Mayor Zamora and Chief Montague rather than to Carlton.

"I think it's a good idea," said Robin Montague. "We have to get that rotting flesh off the beach soon. The merchants are complaining."

"I can understand that," Mayor Zamora said. "This will make even more of the surfers go north to Playa Bonita. And this has to be resolved before the invitational next month." Mayor Zamora was clearly uneasy at the prospect of bad publicity harming the surfing competition he had worked so hard to organize for the Central Hills–Laguna Pequeña area.

"Tom's examination won't take long, and the sooner he gets to it, the sooner the carcass can be disposed of," Mr. Swift said, standing. "Tom, why don't you take Rick with you to help out?"

"I will. And Rob and Orb, too," Tom said, referring to his two robots. The meeting broke up, the tension as thick as ever.

* * *

"Hold your nose," Rick Cantwell choked out. "That carcass is getting really ripe."

"The odor is not unduly affecting sales of food and drink," Orb said. "Business is brisk."

"That's because of Dan Coster. He's always so hungry that he'd eat the rear tire off his car if he couldn't get a burger," Rick said.

"When the novelty wears off, people won't put up with the smell," Tom said. He waved at Dan, who started over from a burger stand. "Unpack the equipment, Rob. And carry Orb on your shoulder."

"That is an excellent position for observation and recording, Tom," said Rob, the gleaming seven-foot-tall robot. Rob lifted the basketball-size Orb onto his shoulder, where the robot clicked down securely onto a magnetic pad. The spherical robot, which contained one of the world's most advanced artificial-intelligence systems, had been designed by Tom to be the brains to Rob's brawn.

"We'll have to work fast," Rick said, holding his nose. "I'm surprised they haven't already dragged the carcass out to sea."

"Yeah, why haven't they gotten rid of this health menace?" a frustrated surfer called out. "This whole place stinks. I'm going up to

Playa Bonita to get in some surfing where the beach is clean."

"Hey, go on and split. That leaves the best beach around for the best surfers," Dan Coster called after him.

"Ah, come on, guys. Let's get some fresh air." The surfer motioned to a tight knot of his friends, and they left.

"That's what'll happen to the invitational if we don't get this cleared up quick," Tom said, trudging through the sand to the police cordon.

"You Tom Swift?" asked a uniformed officer, looking at Orb, Rob, and the equipment the robot carried, before turning back to Tom. "Got a call from Chief Montague saying a tall blond guy was going to examine the thing." The officer jerked his thumb over his shoulder in the direction of the beached monster. "Get to it, will you? Even my dog won't come close to me when I get off duty."

"I won't take long," Tom promised.

"Need any help, Tom?" Dan asked, looking back toward the surf.

"Go practice," Tom said with a smile. "You need it. We'll get this squared away and join you."

Rob, with Orb on his shoulder, and Rick began setting up the test equipment while Tom slowly circled the dead behemoth.

"Here, Rick, we'd better put these on." Tom took out two pairs of small nose filters and handed one to his friend. Anticipating the need, he'd had Rob run them off the night before. He inhaled deeply and got only fresh air without a hint of decaying flesh.

"What do you think of it, Tom?" Rick asked, staring at the carcass. He pressed the side of his nose to get his filters into the proper position.

"It looks like an orca—a killer whale," Tom said. "But I estimate that it's more than fifty feet long. Long strips of flesh are missing in places along its sides, as if it had been rotting before it hit the beach. And there are unusual spiny growths on the head."

"Besides all that," Rick said, "it's downright ugly. Don't expect me to invite it to my next party. Look at that sandpaper skin, will you?"

"I have photographed it all for reference, Tom," Orb piped up.

"Great," Tom said. He was anxious to get to work. "Let's collect some tissue samples."

"Why not let Rob and Orb finish this?" Rick asked. "Do you want to touch that thing any longer than you have to, even with rubber gloves? It's pretty yucky."

"A good point." Tom wasn't squeamish, but he knew the robots would be able to go where he didn't want to. Tom gave instructions to Rob and Orb, including examination of the gas-bloated interior, then prepared the chemicals to test the samples they brought back. He put a thin section of tissue into a compact DNA analyzer he had invented.

"Well?" Rick asked. "What do you make of it?"

For a moment Tom ignored Rick. He spoke quietly to Orb, giving the brainy robot a string of numbers from the analyzer readouts. Orb's external circuits glowed; then it spoke to Tom briefly. Tom nodded and turned back to Rick.

"Its genetic structure indicates that it's definitely an orca," Tom said slowly. "But there's something weird about it."

"Other than being bigger than a house?" asked Rick.

"That's the problem," said Tom. "This orca's no more than six weeks old. It's a baby."

"But it's much bigger than a full-grown killer whale!"

"I know," Tom said in a worried tone. "And I've found traces of genetically engineered growth hormone. After checking the new lab, I was certain that none of my experimental compound could have been released. Now, I'm not so sure—somehow I may be responsible for this monster!"

5

I WAS RIGHT!" TOM SWIFT CRIED. "I KNEW IT!"

"What's that?" asked Rick, wandering around in the Hydro-Projects Wing behind Tom. It was the afternoon, and Rick was munching on the last cold slice of a "large pie with everything."

"It's taken two days of hard work to show the genetically altered hormone did *not* come from my lab," Tom said.

"You can tell that?" Rick was impressed.

"I use a DNA marker to keep track of the plasmids. See, I use a transposon to move bits of the DNA chain. This is different from cutting the chain with a restriction enzyme. It's—"

"Whoa, don't get all cranked up. Either cut to the chase or tell it to George."

"Sorry," Tom said. "I'm getting ahead of myself. The compound that caused the orca to grow so fast came from a source other than the Swift-engineered hormone. And it seems clearly to be a by-product of faulty bioengineering. The strange growth hormone caused rapid growth in the wrong cells. In fact, its composition looks a lot like that of *human* growth hormone."

"You're not playing around with that, are you?"

"There's no reason to. Experiments with hGh, as the big companies call it, are far more difficult and have nothing to do with fish."

"So if you're not on the hook, who is?" Rick walked over to where Rob and Orb were conducting experiments on slimy gray blobs. Rick made a face and turned away.

"I wish I knew. Dumping hGh into the ocean is more than dangerous. It's criminal," Tom said grimly.

"Too bad this business is in that jerk Carlton's court now," Rick said. "He's talking about shutting down the beach at Laguna Pequeña."

"And do you really want to drive north to Playa Bonita to surf?" Tom asked.

Rick laughed. "No way! The waves are no-where near as good."

"I hear you." Tom pushed back from his workbench and closed his lab book. "This is really serious stuff, Rick. The hGh might be causing other problems in the ocean."

"Such as more monsters, like whatever bit Amber?"

"Possibly," Tom said, his mind racing. "I dropped whatever jammed the turbine blade on Dad's tidal generator, but it might have been a bone. A big bone."

"Big like a bone that had been enhanced by a hormone?" Rick let out a low whistle.

"You catch my drift. This could upset the ecology of the entire coast." Tom turned to his computer and called up a simulation that Rob and Orb had input, showing the dangers of dumping hGh in the ocean.

He was interrupted by the phone softly chiming. Tom swung around in his swivel chair and punched a button on his computer keyboard.

"Tom Swift speaking." Tom listened intently, then said, "Be right there." He hit the disconnect button on the console.

"What's up?" Rick asked.

"That was Chief Montague. She wants me to come to Laguna Pequeña right away. She wouldn't say what was wrong, but it sounded serious."

"At least it's not the orca," Rick said. "Mind if I come along?"

Tom shook his head, wondering what was so urgent. The Coast Guard had hauled the orca out to sea the day before. He turned to Rob and Orb and instructed them to go back to the job of genetically engineering pollution-eating bacteria. Then he and Rick got into Tom's van and headed for the beach. Parking wasn't a problem, as the beach lots were nearly deserted.

"I wonder where everyone is," Tom said.

"Flashing red lights attract a crowd, don't they?" Rick said. "I'd say everyone's over there." He pointed down the beach to an ambulance.

Tom and Rick ran over to the emergency vehicle. A dozen people sat on the rocks overlooking the scene, and several police officers held back the few who tried to get too close. Tom saw Chief Montague and waved to her.

"Tom, you got here fast. Good. I got your report on the orca and passed it along to Mayor Zamora. Mitch Carlton also got a copy." She turned and looked toward the edge of the water where two paramedics were working on a swimmer.

"What's going on?" Tom asked. "Something to do with the orca?"

"You tell me. That guy was surfing, practicing for the invitational next month, when he wiped out. Something hit his board and knocked him off."

"I know him," Rick said. "He's not too good. I doubt he'll get past the preliminary round."

"That's not the point. He might not be a great surfer, but he was right on the money about this." Chief Montague held up an ankle cord fastened to a surfboard. She handed it to Tom.

"It's been bitten through," he said, after examining the nylon cord.

"There's a piece taken out of his board, too. The bite radius measures two feet across. That's one big shark—or so I thought," the chief said.

"But now you don't. Why?" Tom asked. "This is pretty good evidence." He held up the ankle cord.

"Because that surfer also came out with blisters all over his arm and a rash where he claims whatever it was rubbed against his leg. Sharks don't cause blisters." Chief Montague shook her head. "This is getting serious. I want to close the beach."

"You can't do that!" cried a tall, slender

man from the edge of the small crowd. "My taco stand is hurting now. Close the beach and I'm out of business!"

Several other merchants from beachfront stores agreed.

"Let me through," came Mitch Carlton's gruff voice. "I think the chief has finally got it right. This entire beach ought to be closed."

"I disagree," Mayor Zamora said. Tom turned and saw the two men, who had come up while he was talking to Chief Montague.

"You're just out to get a few votes and campaign contributions," Carlton accused. "I've got to consider the health and safety of everyone using the Laguna Pequeña beach. I don't care what the merchants association says or how much time you've spent organizing that ridiculous surfing competition."

"It's not that and you know it," Zamora snapped. He calmed himself down and continued. "A single incident does not constitute a health crisis and shouldn't cause needless panic."

"Thanks, Mayor!" called the man who had spoken out against closing the beach. "We don't need to go into bankruptcy just because some kid got banged up."

Carlton ignored the man and spoke to the mayor. "There's been more than one incident, but maybe you're right, Mayor. I hope so, for your sake." Mitch Carlton turned on his heel and stalked off.

"Chief, I'd like a word with you." Hector Zamora took Robin Montague to one side and spoke quietly with her, leaving Rick and Tom alone.

"I want to look at the blisters," Tom said going over to the surfer.

"Nothing serious, guys." The surfer flexed his bandaged arm. "I'll be ready for the invitational—if there is one." He looked out toward the surf and shivered involuntarily.

"Why do you think Carlton gave in so easily?" Rick asked as they walked away. "You and Chief Montague are right. It would be smart to close the beach until this is cleared up."

"Politics," Tom answered. "If Carlton closes the beach without a good reason, he'll look like a jerk. But if he cautions Mayor Zamora to close it and there's any more trouble, it'll be on the mayor's head."

"And Mitch Carlton will look like a hero," Rick finished in disgust. "So what are you going to do?"

"I want to give the entire beach a good going-over." Tom looked up and down the deserted beach and saw Laguna Pequeña's empty future if he didn't come up with some answers.

"It'd be more fun walking the beach if Sandra and Mandy were here," Rick suggested.

"You're right," Tom said, "but let's snoop around, anyway. You go south and I'll go north."

Tom started walking briskly, looking for any trace of mutated fish that might have washed up on the beach. In less than five minutes he heard Rick calling. Tom stopped and turned.

"Tom, come quick!" Rick cried. "It—it's George!"

Tom retraced his path, running to Rick's side. Rick stabbed a finger toward a tidal pool. "When I saw *that*, I thought George had escaped his tank in your lab."

Tom did a double take. For a split second he, too, thought he was looking at his experimental bass. A fish matching George's size and coloration lay in the pool.

"That's not a bass," Tom said, moving closer. He edged down into the shallow pool and waded to the dead fish.

"How did it get into the tidal pool?" Rick asked.

"It must have come in at high tide. Now that the tide's pulling back, it's stranded." Tom knelt and picked up a piece of driftwood to poke at the fish. Remembering the surfer's blisters and rash, he didn't want to touch it with his bare hands.

Rick looked over his friend's shoulder. "Wow, it's got three eyes."

Tom nodded, his expression grim. The beginnings of a third eye in the middle of the fish's head hinted at growth hormone gone berserk. He had worked hard to contain his recombinant DNA product. Someone else hadn't been so careful.

"This fish has to have eaten something with hGh in it." Tom rolled the fish over and made a face.

"Count the fins," Tom said, fascinated and repelled at the same time. "One, two, three, four on one side, and seven on the other. This fish's genes went wild."

"I sure wouldn't want to run into that thing while swimming," Rick said.

"There's something else," Tom said, a lump forming in the pit of his stomach. The implications of the fins shocked him. "It could have slithered into the pool just like an amphibian."

"You mean it used those fins as legs?" Rick looked astounded. "This is evolution at work."

"Not evolution, Rick—mutation," Tom said. The irregular nodules along the dead fish's sides oozed ichorous pus. Tom poked at one, and it broke open, a thick stream of inky juice leaking into the tidal pool.

"You want to take this thing back to your lab?" Rick's tone revealed how uneasy he was about carrying the diseased-looking fish.

"There's no need. I can just take several tissue samples. I can't learn as much about its genetic makeup from dissection as I can by scanning it with an electron microscope." Tom took several small stoppered tubes from his pocket and used his multipurpose pocket knife to get tissue samples.

"Let's get these into the dry-ice cooler in my van," Tom said, "before there's any deterioration."

Tom had left the cooler on the front seat for easy access. He placed the tubes carefully in a rack he had put inside the cooler, then locked the van. As they walked back to the beach to continue their search, Tom shook his head and said, "You know, it's hard to believe that monstrously mutated fish was once a common, inch-long herring."

"What?" Rick cried. "You mean it was one of those nice tasty little fishes we know and love as canned sardines?"

"Yes," said Tom, "in spite of its size, this is a *Clupea harengus pallasi*."

"Remind me never again even to ask for anchovies on a pizza," Rick said with feeling.

"I need to look around some more," Tom said. "Human growth hormone almost certainly is being released into the ocean. I want to find out where it's coming from."

"Well," Rick said, looking out across the waves, "it might be the result of something dumped overboard from a passing ship. You'll never pinpoint the source if that's what happened."

"I'll have Rob check ship routes and manifests. But I really doubt that's where the stuff came from. A much more likely source is a coastal pharmaceutical or bioengineering firm."

"Which one?" Rick asked.

Tom started to reply when an ear-piercing alarm sounded from the parking lot.

"That's my van!" Tom cried. "Someone's trying to break into it!"

Tom and Rick ran for the lot. No one was there, but the van's side door stood open a few inches.

"It doesn't look as if anything's missing," Rick said, examining the front. "The CD player's still there."

"Yeah," Tom said, "but the cooler's gone!"

He heard running feet at the far end of the lot. He shouted to Rick to watch the van, then ran as hard as he could. Tom saw a tall, thin figure pause before getting into a low-slung sports car.

"Stop!" he shouted. The thief ignored him and got into the car.

Tom saw the driver just before the car roared off. He was certain it was the same girl who had taken his picture at the beach party.

Tom ran back to the van and shouted to Rick, "Climb in! We can catch her before she gets too far away."

"Want to bet?" Rick asked, leaning against the van. He pointed to the right front tire. It was flat.

Tom spun and watched the sports car's taillights vanish around a curve in the road. The girl had gotten away, but he was determined to find out what was going on. Someone was illegally dumping genetically engineered growth hormone, with horrible results. If word got out that Tom was experimenting with growth hormone, people would assume that Swift Enterprises was the source of the illegal dumping. Tom knew he had to discover the real source before that happened.

The tissue samples from the mutated herring might have provided the answer, but now they'd been stolen. Tom couldn't shake the sudden thought that he was caught in some hidden conspiracy and was being set up to take the fall.

6

I DON'T KNOW IF WE SHOULD SWIM HERE," Mandy Coster said, eyeing the tranquil waters off Laguna Pequeña beach. "Too much has happened in the past week."

"We have to fight the fear and hysteria that've been growing and show support for the merchants association," Sandra said. "We shouldn't take off for Playa Bonita just because other kids have. Besides, this beach isn't really dangerous, it is, Tom?"

"They would have closed the beach if it was risky, right, Tom?" Rick asked.

The three looked at him for reassurance. Tom considered telling them they ought to join the others at a safer beach, then decided he was being too cautious. He had quickly tested a water sample and found no harmful man-made chemicals.

"As far as I can tell," Tom said slowly, "the water is safe—for now."

"I vote we check out the waves," Rick said with a laugh. He ran for the water and splashed into the surf, then dived cleanly, swimming away. Sandra followed. Mandy hesitated, looking to Tom for encouragement.

Tom saw her look and broke into a reassuring grin. "I don't want Rick and Sandra to have all the fun. Let's go!" With that, Tom dashed off to catch an incoming wave. Within five minutes any misgivings he'd had were long gone.

Tom admitted to himself that the cause of the marine mutations might be miles and miles away. Freak currents could have washed the mutant fish onto the beach.

"Where's Rick?" Sandra called. "He was—" She let out a yelp and slid under the water, only to resurface again seconds later. She sputtered and spit water.

Rick bobbed up a few feet from her. "Gotcha!" he cried.

"You miserable, stinking piece of fish bait!" Sandra shouted. "You grabbed me!"

"Don't be such a spoilsport," Rick told her. "We're supposed to be enjoying ourselves."

"Tom!" Mandy shrieked. "How could you?"

"What are you talking about?" Tom paddled around in the water a few yards away from Mandy.

"I expect Rick to clown around, but not you!"

"Oh, really? You think I can't?" Tom protested, assuming that Mandy was joking. He had started for Mandy when she threw her arms up in the air and twisted violently.

Tom saw her go under—and then saw why. A long tentacle shot toward her. Thicker than Tom's arm, the rubbery tentacle lashed around, reaching high out of the water. As it slapped down, Mandy wrenched free and struggled toward the surface.

Tom swam hard and put himself between Mandy and the tentacle.

"Swim for shore, Mandy. Hurry!" Tom cried. A slippery appendage groped for his leg.

"Don't try to fight it, Tom," Mandy gasped. "It's too strong!"

When Tom saw that Mandy was close to shore, he dived, groping for the creature that had tried to pull Mandy under. But now the beast was swimming up, coming straight for *him!*

Tom turned in the water and felt something

slimy slide past his arm. Then stinging pain hit him like a tidal wave.

Fighting to get to the surface, Tom kicked out. His lungs turned to liquid fire from lack of oxygen as a steely noose clamped itself securely around his ankle, keeping him down. He kicked harder and felt squishy flesh under his foot. He kept kicking until the burning ran all the way up his leg.

Just when he thought he couldn't take any more, Tom tensed for one last effort. He reached down and grabbed at the beast holding him. Fingers clawing, he punished the creature.

Then, as suddenly as he had been pulled under, he was propelled to the surface. The submerged monster had finally let him go.

Tom floated on his back, gasping for air. He felt something on his arms and thrashed around until he heard Rick's voice.

"Stop fighting me, Tom. We're trying to get you to the beach."

Tom saw his friend on one side and Sandra on the other. He relaxed and let them tow him until he regained enough strength to swim on his own. When his feet hit the sand, he struggled to stand. He glanced down and saw that his leg and hand were blistered.

He looked back into the water and saw a shadowy shape looming in the depths. The dark mass veered off and vanished back into the ocean. Tom sank down on the beach and shivered.

"This has been one rotten afternoon," Sandra said, sitting beside Tom on the couch in the Swift family living room. Mandy and Rick sat in separate chairs on either side of the couch.

"I was wrong about Laguna Pequeña, I guess," Tom said. Worse than being wrong was being jumped on by Mitch Carlton when he reported their injuries. Tom had used a special ointment from his first-aid kit to treat his and Mandy's minor burns and blisters. To treat the more serious burns on Tom's arm and leg, they had driven back to the main complex of Swift Enterprises. There Tom was able to use one of his recent inventions—artificial skin, which he applied in layers and wrapped. After twenty-four hours it would be a permanent part of his skin.

"I can't believe the way Carlton brought in the police and immediately cordoned off the beach," Rick said. "He made me feel like a criminal."

"He didn't care about us," Sandra said. "All he wanted to do was play up to the press that he had warned Mayor Zamora about the danger."

"The beach won't be closed long," Tom predicted.

"Look, there's Mayor Zamora," Sandra said, turning on the TV news. "He's down at the beach."

Tom leaned forward, listening to what the mayor had to say.

"The beach will be closed for evaluation," Mayor Zamora told the reporter. He looked nervous, glancing off-camera several times. Before he could say more, the reporter cut to Mitch Carlton.

"Mr. Carlton," she asked, "what steps are you taking to find the cause of the injuries reported by swimmers today and earlier this week?"

Carlton grabbed the microphone and pulled it closer. He cleared his throat as if getting ready to make a long speech. "I warned Mayor Zamora about the severe danger, but he ignored me," he said. "I favored closing Laguna Pequeña after the mutated orca washed up and posed a major hazard to public health."

"Will you shut other beaches as well?" the reporter asked.

"This is the only one requiring such drastic measures. Playa Bonita will remain open."

"What is causing these mutant fish to come into the bay?" The reporter fought to get the mike back. Carlton clung to it, not wanting to give up his chance to be on TV.

"We're looking into several possible causes now," Carlton said. The reporter yanked the mike out of his hand and went to a break.

"I know what's coming," Tom said glumly.

"Tom, they couldn't possibly think that you're in any way—" Before Mandy could say anything else, she was cut off by Rick.

"Shhh! They're back with the news," Rick said, leaning forward in his chair.

"This reporter has just received an anonymous tip that Swift Enterprises is responsible for illegal dumping of genetically active material. Can you comment on this, Mr. Carlton?"

"I don't know if Swift Enterprises is at fault. They've always been responsive to environmental concerns," Carlton said. "But it is possible, since they are involved in genetic-engineering research."

"Would this explain the mutated fish and burn injuries to swimmers at Laguna Pequeña beach?"

"Perhaps, but it's certainly too soon to draw conclusions," Carlton said. "But I do intend to pursue this until the truth comes out."

"Let me say a word," Mayor Zamora cut in. "I know Mr. Swift and many of the other top scientists at Swift Enterprises. They would never allow such a thing to happen." The camera panned toward him but stopped when the reporter spoke again.

"This is Cynthia Arnold at Laguna Pequeña. Back to the studio." The scene shifted to the news anchors.

"We'll bring you more on this fast-breaking story tonight at eleven," one anchor promised. The other started the lead-in for the weather.

"They actually accused us of being responsible!" Sandra raged.

Before Tom could reply, Mr. Swift came in. "Who's accused of doing what?" he asked, dropping his briefcase on the hall table. He came into the living room and saw the weather forecaster pointing to a map of the United States. "Don't tell me we're responsible for the weather?" He laughed at this, but the others did not.

"Somebody called the TV station and said we were responsible for the mutations down at Laguna Pequeña beach, Dad," Tom explained. "They claimed we were dumping genetically active material."

"This isn't a joke, is it?" Mr. Swift looked at his son and daughter. "Who said that?"

"It was an anonymous tip," Sandra said.

"This is terribly serious," Mr. Swift said.

"Accusations like this are hard to answer, but there's no need to get so worked up. I'll get in touch with the reporter. Who was it?"

"Cynthia Arnold."

"I'll call Ms. Arnold and take care of everything. Now, what's for supper? I'm famished. Rick, Mandy, you can stay for dinner, if you'd like."

Both Rick and Mandy begged off and left.

The Swift family went to eat, but Tom's mind returned to the accusations about the growth hormone. His father might not take them seriously, but he did.

Tom Swift had everything he needed for sampling the water along the Laguna Pequeña shore. His knowing that Swift Enterprises was innocent meant nothing—he had to *prove* it, and he would.

He slipped out of the house and drove his van toward the front gate of the company complex. It was just after 10:00 P.M. when he pulled up by the security gate. Chief of Security Harlan Ames came over to the van.

"I was going to call," Harlan said. "Protesters began showing up after the six o'clock news. At first it was two or three, but the crowd's been growing."

"Maybe I can talk to them," Tom suggested.

"Why don't you let your father handle this," Harlan said.

"Well, can I get out the side gate?"

"I'll check." Harlan Ames spoke quickly into his walkie-talkie, then nodded to Tom. "I'm going to get your father down here. It won't be long before the TV reporters start swarming to get a story on the eleven o'clock news. An official statement has to be ready."

"Thanks, Harlan," Tom said. He wheeled the van around and drove to a gate about a mile farther along the security fence. No protesters had gathered there, and Tom passed through without a problem.

When he arrived at Laguna Pequeña, the beach was very quiet. Few swimmers usually came out at this time of night, and the beach officially closed at eleven, but no one was even walking along the shore. Tom parked, noticing only one other car at the far end of the lot.

After quickly assembling his water sampling equipment, he hurried to the beach. Time was turning into an enemy. Tom took water samples along the beach where the orca had washed up, then began working south, taking a sample every hundred yards. When he had worked his way all around the curving bay to the south, he started north, retracing his steps.

A few minutes later Tom heard sand crunching softly behind him. He turned and saw the tall, thin girl who had taken his picture repeatedly at the beach party. She had the camera slung around her neck.

"Do you want to take my picture again?" Tom asked, facing her. He wondered if she would run away as she had at the party.

"What are you doing?" she asked, sounding as if she thought Tom was committing a crime.

"Something is causing the mutation of marine life along the beach. I want to find the source of the genetically altered material causing the mutations. I'm taking samples in an attempt to track it down."

"You don't know where it's coming from?" She seemed surprised and a little flustered. Then she stiffened. "You're lying."

Tom took a closer look at her. She was about his age, though he didn't remember seeing her at Jefferson High. Her long hair rippled in dark waves from the sea breeze, and she moved with the controlled grace of a gymnast as she started to go.

"Wait," Tom said. He took the bag with the ocean samples off his shoulder and let it rest on the sand. "I'm Tom Swift, but I get the feeling you know that already. And you punctured the tire on my van the other night, didn't you?"

"Sorry about that," she said, not bothering to deny it. "I didn't want you to follow me."

"Why do you think I'm lying about the source of the growth hormone?" Tom was taken by her beauty as well as dismayed by her insistence that he was lying. "Why have you been trailing me?"

"I wanted to see the famous Tom Swift," the girl replied. "And clearly you *are* responsible for dumping the hGh into the ocean." She pointed toward the promontory where the Hydro-Projects Wing was situated.

"Swift Enterprises isn't responsible," Tom said, "and you seem to know a lot about it. Why did you say *human* growth hormone is causing the problems? Who are you, anyway? A reporter?"

"My name is Melanie." She shifted from foot to foot. "I have to leave," she said suddenly, then turned and ran off.

"Wait!" Tom called. He ran after her but got only a few yards before remembering his bag with the water samples. He hesitated, then dashed back and grabbed his bag, but Melanie kept running.

When he got to the parking lot, he heard a roar from a sports car and saw taillights vanishing around the curve in the road. He was frustrated and torn by conflicting emotions. On the one hand, he wouldn't mind getting to know her better. On the other hand, she had accused him of dangerous illegal activity. Tom's intuition told him that either she was responsible for the anonymous tip to the TV station or she knew who was. Whatever her game, it could easily put Tom and his family in serious legal trouble. More than ever he was determined to find out who she was—and what he might have done to make her his enemy.

7

ANOTHER SLEEPLESS NIGHT, TOM THOUGHT. He yawned as he walked toward the administration building of Swift Enterprises. He had spent the night running tests on the water samples he had gathered—and thinking.

After the TV news report a lot of people in Central Hills would believe that Swift Enterprises had dumped the genetically active material into the ocean. Tom didn't know anything about Melanie, but it bothered him that she might have been responsible for spreading the lie.

But he now had the information he had sought. Or part of it, at least. The concentration of hGh in the ocean samples increased the farther south Tom had gone, showing Swift Enterprises was not responsible. All water discharge from Swift Enterprises was to the north.

This left one big question: who was responsible? Tom wanted to talk with his father about this right away. He took the elevator to the top floor and greeted the receptionist.

"Your father is with an official from the Environmental Protection Agency," Mary Ann Jennings said.

"Does he need me there?"

"It doesn't seem so," said Mitch Carlton. Tom spun around, surprised. The public health director had come out of Mr. Swift's office. "The EPA is asking the hard questions now. You'd only get in the way."

"Dad can answer any charge. We're innocent."

"How do you account for that tip to the TV station?"

"Who made it? I heard it was anonymous." Tom didn't like the sneer on Mitch Carlton's face.

Carlton shrugged off Tom's objection. "It might have been somebody who works here and doesn't want to get fired for blowing the whistle on you. I'm calling for a full public investigation of your waste disposal practices."

"Go ahead. We have nothing to hide," Tom said. He started to tell Carlton that he had discovered higher concentrations of hGh to the south, then held back. Tom wasn't sure the director wanted facts. Saving the test results for the EPA might be a better idea.

"You may have Mayor Zamora in your pocket, but I can take you on and win. There won't be a Swift Enterprises left when this is put before the public," Carlton said.

"Are you more interested in serving the public or in getting elected mayor, Mr. Carlton?" Tom asked.

Carlton stiffened and pressed his lips into a thin line. "I don't have to listen to a kid who's still wet behind the ears," he snapped. Then he stalked out of the reception area.

"Whew," said Mary Ann. "He's getting to be unbearable. I'd never vote for him."

"Glad to hear it. Neither would I." Tom looked toward the closed door to his father's office. "I don't want to barge in. Tell Dad I'll be out at the Hydro-Projects Wing, doing some work."

"All right, Tom." Mary Ann tried to put on a cheerful expression but failed. That didn't lighten Tom's mood as he left for his new lab.

Tom worked steadily, putting all of his water samples through the computerized analyzer to get a DNA "fingerprint" of the mysterious hGh. He then made comparisons with his own genetically engineered hormone, noting the differences. He now had strong evidence in Swift Enterprises' favor, and he thought it would convince any panel of impartial EPA scientists.

"Rob, set up the nutrient containers. We're ready to get going."

"On which experiment, Tom?" the towering robot asked. Rob moved to obey even as he asked his question.

"I'm preparing the program for Orb right now. You're going to look for the right gene combination to create bacteria that will eat the hGh being discharged along Laguna Pequeña beach."

"The equipment will be ready in a few minutes, Tom," Rob answered.

"Don't worry, Tom. We can take care of this for you. Do you have the new program ready?" Orb said, glowing on the workbench next to the nutrient solution.

"Just a second, Orb. Okay—here it comes." Tom pushed a small floppy disk into Orb's input slot. Orb whirred and purred, digesting the electronic data.

Tom looked up when he heard the outer door chime, alerting him to a visitor. He touched the button that changed the screen on his monitor from a computer readout to a camera view of the front. Tom immediately hit the intercom button.

"Mandy!" he said, brightening. "It's good to see you. I wasn't expecting you."

"Mary Ann Jennings told me you were here and that it would be all right for me to stop by," she said, looking up at the camera.

"Come on in." Tom keyed in the computer code to open the exterior door. He went to his lab door and opened it just as Mandy crossed the lobby.

"You know you can always visit," Tom said. "How's your leg?"

"It's fine. That burn ointment of yours worked well." Mandy fell silent.

"Good," Tom said. He licked his lips. "Mandy, look, I've been so busy lately it seems as if I'm ignoring you. I'm not."

"Tom," Mandy said softly, "I want to apologize. I blamed you for a lot of things that weren't your fault. You'd never allow the illegal dumping of that gunk, and if it happened by accident, you would never try to cover it up, as they're saying on TV."

"That's okay," Tom said, relieved that Mandy believed him. Hesitantly he took her hand. Mandy moved closer. So did Tom—just as the front door opened. Tom and Mandy jumped back. Mr. Swift walked briskly across the lobby to where they stood, just outside Tom's lab.

"Tom, glad I caught you. Hello, Mandy," Mr. Swift said with a quick nod in her direction. "I've just come from a meeting with the EPA."

"How did it go?" Tom asked.

"A team of experts is being assembled now. It'll be a few days before they arrive." Mr. Swift tried to look confident, but Tom saw tiny worry lines around his father's eyes.

"I'm about finished putting together the evidence," Tom said. "I'm certain that the genetically active material is being dumped through sewage pipes from the new Southside Industrial Complex."

Mr. Swift heaved a sigh of relief. "That's good news. I haven't paid much attention to the companies going in there. Have you, Tom?"

"There must be ten or twelve of them," Tom said. "I don't remember seeing a biotech company. But I've been too busy to check out the sort of work that all of them are currently engaged in."

"Find the responsible party. And put all hard evidence into Megatron's database. I've agreed to be interviewed by Cynthia Arnold on the evening news to get this out in the open."

Mr. Swift started out, then paused and turned to Mandy. "Can you come with me, Mandy? Sandra wants to see you. She's over at our house, and Tom needs to get that data ready as soon as possible."

"I understand," Mandy said. She gave Tom a bright smile, then left with Mr. Swift.

Tom went back into his lab and saw that Rob and Orb had already begun to genetically engineer the bacteria that would eat the illegally dumped hGh. Finally, he thought, we're on top of the situation. I'll give Dad the evidence to clear us, the new bacteria will clean up the hGh, and Laguna Pequeña can return to normal.

Tom, Sandra, and Mrs. Swift sat comfortably in their living room, waiting for the commercials to end and the six o'clock news to begin.

"Do you think Dad will be the lead story on the news?" Sandra asked. Tom nodded, his mind racing. He was sure he had given his father all the information he could. But now doubt crept into his mind. Would it be enough to convince the reporter and everyone watching the news that Swift Enterprises had no part in the contamination causing the marine mutations? Truth wasn't something that communicated well in snappy ten-second sound bites.

"I think it will be the top story," Mrs. Swift said. "This is important to everyone in Central Hills."

"Are they still talking about canceling the surfing invitational?" Tom asked.

"If that Mitch Carlton had his way, he'd put up a quarantine," Sandra said, incensed. "He wants to put a lid on Laguna Pequeña and nail it down for months!"

"There's your father," Mrs. Swift said. She tried to keep calm, but Tom saw his mother was as upset about Mitch Carlton's claims as he was.

"With us this evening is the president of Swift Enterprises, Thomas Swift, Sr. Mr. Swift," Cynthia Arnold said, "when do you propose to stop dumping dangerous DNA material into Laguna Pequeña?"

"That's not fair!" Tom cried. "She's accusing him of doing something we never did."

"She might as well ask him if he still beats his dog," Sandra grumbled.

Tom was relieved that his father kept his cool in spite of the reporter's tone.

"Swift Enterprises has never conducted such dumping. My son, Tom, has prepared evidence showing—"

Mr. Swift wasn't allowed to finish. Mitch

Carlton crowded into the picture. The camera panned to the director of public health.

"I have important evidence that has significant bearing on this," Carlton said.

"What is it, Mr. Carlton?" Cynthia Arnold asked.

"Mr. Swift's company is engaged in genetic research. Do you deny that?"

Mr. Swift shook his head. "Of course I don't deny it. We're a leader in the field. My son, Tom, is in charge of the bioengineered fish-growth hormone experiment."

"Mr. Swift," Cynthia Arnold said, "are you admitting that your own son is responsible for the growth hormone in the bay?"

"Not at all," Mr. Swift said. He was starting to sound angry.

"No, Dad, don't let them goad you into saying anything more," Tom pleaded. He knew his father had nothing to hide, but the reporter was starting to distort his answers, and Mitch Carlton was helping her.

"The orca was mutated due to a bioengineered growth hormone like the one your son is working on," Carlton stated. "Do you deny that?"

"It's not ours," Mr. Swift said, almost spitting out the words. "We work on many cutting-edge projects, and we maintain strict safety procedures.

"Isn't it true," Cynthia Arnold asked, "that Swift Enterprises has recently developed an experimental deep-sea oil-drilling platform that will make it easier to drill for offshore oil, further endangering the fragile coastal ecology?"

"Yes, it's true that we have perfected an advanced platform," Mr. Swift started to say. "But we designed it to protect the crews and for—"

"Thomas Swift and Swift Enterprises care nothing for public safety," Mitch Carlton interrupted. "And I have proof of that."

"What proof, Mr. Carlton?" Cynthia Arnold asked.

Carlton cleared his throat dramatically and then announced, "Because of his friendship with Mr. Swift, Mayor Zamora has refused to act to stop this dangerous situation. I can no longer sit idly by. Tomorrow morning I will ask the court for a restraining order preventing any bioengineering research activity at Swift Enterprises until this dangerous situation is resolved. The new experimental wing of Swift Enterprises will be shut down indefinitely."

"You can't do that without any proof!" Mr. Swift was shouting now.

"Here is my proof. Pictures don't lie. I have photos of your son putting the growth hor-

mone into the water at Laguna Pequeña!''
Mitch Carlton held up pictures of Tom taking
water samples the night before.

Tom stared at the screen, unable to speak.
It was his worst nightmare turned horribly
real.

8

I CAN'T BELIEVE IT," RICK CANTWELL SAID, STARing out the van's window. "Carlton never bothered to check what was going on before he showed those photos of you."

"Nobody listened to Mayor Zamora when he pointed out that the pictures proved nothing," Tom said. He tried to put the photos out his mind, but it was hard. Melanie had to have taken them, but why had she given them to Carlton?

"Is there a pizza joint around here?" Rick asked, craning his neck out the window. "It's been five hours since dinner."

In that time Tom had been cruising around the new industrial complex, intent on pinpointing the source of the growth hormone causing the marine mutation.

"This is just an industrial park," Tom said. "This late at night we won't find anything open around here."

"I never realized this area had been built up like this," Rick said, staring at the huge discharge pipes running into the main sewer system from the Southside Industrial complex.

"I know," Tom said. "It's hard to believe this whole area was coastal wetlands before the zoning was changed to allow industrial development." He shook his head in dismay.

Tom checked his map again, using a small flashlight. He and Rick were eight miles down the coast from Laguna Pequeña and almost ten miles away from the Swift Enterprises discharge pipes.

"These businesses sprang up like toadstools after a rain," Tom said, studying the single-story brick buildings. Most of the companies sported high-tech names, but nothing he could associate with genetic engineering.

Tom had eliminated almost all the businesses in the complex as possible sources for the hormone dumping. The only one left was a little farther along the main sewer system.

"That's a creepy-looking place," Rick said, pointing to the large concrete building. "The sign says Loew Industries Desalination Plant.''

Tom used an infrared viewer to get a better look, since the only light in the complex shone directly on the sign. There weren't any windows, and only a few doors interrupted the stark concrete walls.

"You wait here," Tom said. "It's a long shot, but I'm going down to take a sample of the waste water flowing from that exit pipe." He could see it plainly through the viewer, about thirty yards away. Tom scuttled down an incline, made sure no security guards were watching, and took out a small stoppered bottle. He filled it quickly and returned to where Rick was waiting.

"The grounds are barren. They sure don't believe in landscaping," Tom said. "Other companies out here have fences, but nothing this tall, or with electrified wire—I saw the insulators along the top. And the only identification is on the sign. If this is an ocean water desalination plant," Tom said, "why isn't it built out over the ocean?"

"I don't see any big pipes going into the plant, either. You'd think they'd have a pump station to bring in the ocean water," Rick said.

"Those pipes might be underground, but that's expensive for the size of the pipes they'd need." Tom had the feeling Loew Industries did something other than what their sign indicated. A little voice in the back of his head told him that he was missing some obvious fact, but he couldn't pin it down. As he thought about it, he placed a small sample of the waste water in the portable analyzer he'd brought with him.

"Sure is quiet, too," Rick said.

"That's it!" Tom was now certain that something was wrong. "Heavy equipment like pumps, even inside a thick-walled concrete building, would make a lot of noise."

"They might have shut down for the night," Rick pointed out. "It's after eleven."

"Or there might not be any pumps at all getting water from the ocean. I don't see any high-power electrical lines going into the plant." The more Tom studied the grounds, the more certain he was that something other than water desalination went on in there.

Tom's analyzer beeped, startling them both. He looked at the readout and let out a low whistle. "We've found the source, Rick."

"So what are we waiting for?" Rick asked. "Let's go find out why they're dumping that renegade growth hormone gunk."

Tom hesitated. To slip over the high cyclone fence was trespassing, he knew, but it was the best way to find the source of the

hGh. If he waited for the plant to open in the morning, he didn't think anyone would admit to illegal dumping. He needed proof.

"Let's do it," Tom said. They returned to the van to store his equipment. Then Tom took out some thick wires with alligator clips attached. "Be careful of the fence until I do a work-around on the charged wires."

They walked along the tall fence until Tom was satisfied he'd found a good place to enter.

"This'll only take a minute," he told Rick. Tom quickly attached jumpers to the charged wires, disabling them without sending a signal that the wires had been cut.

He took a deep breath. "Let's go," he said, climbing over the fence. Rick followed. They dashed across the barren grounds to the huge concrete building.

"They sure don't worry about decorating, do they?" Rick asked, staring at the rough wall. "And look—"

Tom saw a dark shadow moving behind Rick. He started to call out a warning, but his cry was cut off when a heavy blow knocked him to the ground. A second jolt turned the world black, and Tom lost consciousness.

A nagging ache brought Tom back to his senses and caused him to rub the back of his neck and then his scalp. He winced when he found a large goose egg near the top of his head. It took him several seconds to remember what had happened. Even so, he didn't know how he had come to be sitting in a large overstuffed chair.

"Rick!" he cried, looking around. To his surprise, he was alone in a well-lit large office, its walls lined with hundreds of reference books. An oak desk dominated one side of the room. Tom swung around. There were no windows, and the floor was unadorned gray concrete. He went to the door and gingerly tried the knob.

"Locked," he said softly. He was apparently being held prisoner until someone in authority came for him. Tom knew that might be the police.

He went to the desk and found the drawers locked. A few papers, all signed by a Dr. Lawrence Loew, were scattered on the top. Tom scanned them and found nothing of interest. He turned to the books. He recognized all of the current textbooks on biochemistry and genetic engineering. He searched along the shelves and found an entire section on endocrinology, the science of glands dealing with growth.

Tom frowned when he saw a misplaced book. A copy of *Who's Who in Science* was stuck in the middle of the shelf of medical books. On impulse Tom took it down and flipped through it, looking for Dr. Loew.

He had never heard of Loew, in spite of the man's listed credentials. Tom studied the biography and decided that was because Loew's major accomplishments were more than ten years old. In a rapidly changing field like bioengineering, anything more than a year old was out of date.

Tom looked up when he heard a key in the lock. He put the book back just as a man hardly five feet tall burst into the room.

"Meddler! Trespasser! I'll have you thrown in jail!" the man ranted. He had a broad face and wrinkled yellowish skin that hinted at some serious ailment. Tom was no medical doctor, but he had seen patients with liver disease who had the same jaundiced appearance. What puzzled him most was the man's mouth. Something was wrong about it, but he couldn't figure out what.

"I'm sorry," Tom apologized. "My friend and I—"

"You think you're so smart. What do you know?" the man shouted. "I am Dr. Lawrence Loew, the greatest scientist of our era!"

"I saw your biography in *Who's Who*. It's impressive," Tom said, hoping to calm the man. Dr. Loew's eyes burned with a frightening intensity, and a facial tic twisted his face into a macabre mask.

"You're Tom Swift, and you know it all, don't you?" Dr. Loew rushed over and began shoving Tom with short but powerful arms. Tom dodged back, afraid the man might totally lose control. "You steal the best contracts, and why? For no reason except that you are big."

"Swift Enterprises *is* one of the larger research companies in California," Tom replied. "But the government contracts Swift Enterprises holds were all open to competitive bids. We won because we're the best, not because we're the largest."

"You don't understand," raged Dr. Loew. "I'm talking about sizism. That's what wrong with this country. But I'll show you!" Again he came at Tom. This time his hands were balled into fists. A tiny bit of spittle formed at the corner of his mouth, and his eyes blazed with anger.

"I don't know what you mean," Tom said, backing away. "I came here to find out who was illegally dumping human growth hormone into the waste water system. It's draining into Laguna Pequeña and—"

Tom ducked as Dr. Loew threw a book at him. A second volume followed quickly. Tom put up his hands to keep from being struck.

Dr. Loew raged on, his thin hair flying in wild disarray and his facial tic more pronounced. Every twitch contorted his face into an expression of incredible malice.

"You and your kind are responsible. Sizists!" Dr. Loew swept the papers from his desk with his arm and jumped on top of it with a lithe movement.

Tom circled the room, heading for the door. He wanted to reach the hall outside the office. From there he could make a run for it. But as he reached for the doorknob, the door swung inward and someone entered. Tom stepped back in surprise.

"Melanie!" Tom exclaimed. "What are you doing here?"

She ignored him and spoke instead to Dr. Loew. "I'll take care of him," she said. Behind her two men in white lab coats came in and seized Tom. He struggled but couldn't fight free.

"You will?" Dr. Loew asked. Then, as suddenly as his rage had begun, he became quiet. He nodded at Melanie. "Yes, yes, get him out of here."

The two men with Melanie pulled Tom from the office. He let them drag him along the hall until Melanie hurried up to walk beside him.

"What's going on?" Tom demanded. "You can't just—"

"I don't want to do this," Melanie told him, "but you leave me no choice." To the men she said, "Be sure he leaves the grounds." Then she walked off without so much as a look back. Tom fought harder against the steely hands holding him firmly.

"Melanie!" he shouted. "Where's Rick?" Tom's plea echoed down the hall. The girl had returned to Dr. Loew's office and shut the door. He wasn't sure she had heard him.

"We don't want the kid going to the cops," one man said.

"No way," the other agreed. He motioned toward a room off the hall. They dragged Tom into the room and slammed him hard against the wall. One opened a small first-aid kit and took out a syringe while the other pinned Tom down.

"This won't hurt at all," the white-coated man said, slipping the needle into Tom's arm.

Tom fought the warm sleepy feeling spreading through his body, but to no avail. It quickly left him so weak he couldn't stand up. The world swirled around Tom in a crazy-quilt pattern, and for the second time that evening he passed out.

9

RICK CANTWELL FOUGHT AGAINST THE BROAD leather straps holding him to the table, but he couldn't get free. He squinted into the bright light shining in his face, then turned his head and tried to see something of the room where he was imprisoned.

For a wild moment he thought he was in Tom's lab back at the Hydro-Projects Wing. Then he saw the cluttered tables and dirty test tubes—no way could this be his friend's lab.

Straining, Rick peered down the side of the table and out an open door into an office. He heard the outer door open and people come in. A short man paced back and forth, but

Rick couldn't get a good look at him. The other two men, whom Rick took to be research assistants from their lab coats, stood silent as the short man raged.

"I shouldn't have let him go, but that doesn't matter," the man grumbled. "We have his friend."

"We can't—" one assistant began.

The short man shouted him down. "I need human guinea pigs! Use him to test the next formula. I'll get my revenge on the Swifts through their friend!" The man made some incoherent noises, then spun and stormed from the room.

Rick saw a look of relief on the faces of the two men. Then he went cold inside when he heard one say, "We'd better get to work on the kid. You know how Dr. Loew is."

"It's one thing if he wants to test his growth hormone on himself," the second assistant protested, "but to use some strange kid who happened to be trespassing? That's not right."

"Do *you* want to cross Loew? He might decide to experiment on us, especially when he finds we dumped Swift in his van."

"Hey, you guys don't have to do anything to keep me quiet," Rick called. "I won't let out a peep if you let me go."

"You won't let out a peep if we *don't* let

you go," one assistant said, coming into the lab. "We've got our orders." He went to a cabinet and began taking out racks of test tubes.

"This isn't legal. It's not ethical. How can you experiment on a human being?" Rick objected. He continued to fight the straps, but they held securely.

"I'm ready with the test equipment," one of the men said. "Is the new formula ready?"

"What's going on?" came a cold voice. Rick craned his neck and saw a girl standing in the doorway, her hands on her hips. "You can't hold him like this."

"Please, Miss Loew, your father said—" the other man started to say.

The girl's lips thinned to a determined line. "What happened to Tom Swift?"

The two men exchanged a quick glance. "We did what you told us. We made sure he got back to Swift Enterprises. He's been there an hour already."

"You didn't hurt him?" Rick demanded. The three ignored him.

"Now see that his friend is also returned," the girl told them.

"We can't. Your father's given orders to the contrary." The research assistant looked uncomfortable.

"You probably misunderstood his instructions, Mr. Carter. Go ask him, to be certain.

He's in his office. Both of you." She tapped her foot, waiting for them to leave. "I'll watch this one. Go on."

The two men left.

"What's going on? They're going to experiment on me!" Rick cried.

"Nonsense, they wouldn't do that." The girl looked into the outer office, then quickly unfastened Rick's straps. "I'll show you off the grounds. Don't come back."

Rick followed the girl out of the building to a gate in the tall perimeter fence. She used a small key to open the padlock and held the gate open.

"You're the girl who's been following Tom, aren't you?" Rick asked.

She looked uncomfortable at this. "Please go. Some things here are totally out of control. You can't possibly imagine any of it. It—it's my problem." She bit her lower lip and looked upset.

"Can Tom help? He's a real genius when it comes to technical stuff. And that's what this is all about, isn't it?"

The girl took a quick breath, held it for a few seconds, and then released it in a gust. "Tell Tom I'm sorry for all that's happened. I think I might have misjudged him, but I—" She looked over her shoulder in the direction of the concrete building. A man's strident voice rang out. "Go. Hurry," the girl ordered.

She pushed Rick through the gate and closed it behind him. Then she dashed back to the building. Rick rattled the gate, but it was securely locked.

"Hey, wait! I don't have any way to get home!" But the girl had vanished. Rick looked for Tom's van, but it, and his friend, were gone. He started walking, getting angrier with every step.

Tom had driven off and left him!

Tom Swift's head threatened to split apart from the pain rocketing through it. He moaned, turning slightly, and fell out of the open door of his van, onto the ground. The shock of landing brought him out of his stupor.

Where am I? Tom wondered, sitting up. He put his back to the front wheel of the van. Reaching up, he pressed his hand against the side of the engine hood. He didn't remember what had happened, but he had been here long enough for the engine to cool off.

Tom struggled to his feet, stumbled, and managed to regain his balance. His head pounded harder than ever, and his vision began to blur.

"Home. Got to go home." In the dark Tom

tried to focus his eyes long enough to see what time it was. His wristwatch swam in a red haze of pain as his headache increased. Struggling, he climbed back into the van.

He tried to find his miniphone, but his hands refused to work right. His fingers felt as if they had turned into great, greasy sausages. Tom leaned back, closed his eyes, concentrated, then opened them again. All right, he told himself. I know this road, and it'll take me home. I'll just drive slow and easy.

The van kicked over on the first twist of the ignition key. After a few minutes Tom saw a building complex that he recognized. He steered toward the side gate, thinking he had made it back home. The gate opened automatically, and Tom drove through. Suddenly his vision cleared, and he realized he had taken a wrong turn. He was at the Hydro-Projects Wing.

"Have to get in there, call home. Rob and Orb can help. Someone can help me." Tom tried to remember something important and couldn't. Pain sizzled and popped behind his eyes. His vision began to blur again, but he concentrated and brought the van to a halt in the parking lot. He sat there, trying to remember what was going on.

"Melanie," he said. "She was there. But where?" He held his head. Flashes of memory forced themselves on him, but the pieces wouldn't come together.

He got out of the van and was refreshed by a cool sea breeze. It pushed back some of the pain and let him think better. He walked to the edge of the parking lot and stood beside a low rock wall, reveling in the soothing touch of air blowing past him.

Tom sucked in his breath and listened to the waves pounding against the beach. Then he opened his eyes and stared. The path curled off to his left, and below him was a long drop onto jagged rocks.

Tom wobbled, pain coming in wavering torrents. He thought he heard someone calling to him from far off, but he couldn't be sure. He turned to look, lost his balance, and stumbled—right over the edge of the retaining wall.

10

TOM REELED AND PITCHED HEADFIRST TOWARD the rocks below.

"Tom!" The voice came from a million miles off, but the hand on the waistband of his jeans held secure. As Tom dangled over the wall, the blood rushing to his head, he thought he recognized the voice.

"Rick?" he asked. "Is that you?"

"It's me, all right," came Rick's answer. "But I can't hang on to you forever. Push yourself up."

Tom did as his friend asked, pressing his palms against the rough rocks so Rick could haul him up.

"What were you thinking of?" Rick demanded, panting harshly. "You could have been killed."

"I don't know where I am," Tom said, looking around. "There was something important I had to do. You were part of it. I remember that much."

"They did something nasty to you, Tom. Come on, old buddy. Let me get you into your lab so you can lie down and I can use the phone. You need more help than I can give you."

Rick draped Tom's left arm over his shoulder and with his right arm supported Tom up the steps and into the Hydro-Projects Wing. He deposited Tom in the chair in front of his computer terminal while he called Mr. Swift. Fifteen minutes later Mr. Swift and a Swift Enterprises medical doctor arrived.

"He's coming out of it," Dr. Yukawa said after examining Tom carefully, "although I'm not sure what they gave him."

"I don't remember much," Tom said, "but bits and pieces are coming back."

"You rest, Tom," Mr. Swift urged.

"I agree," the doctor said. "In a few hours, you should begin to remember things. I don't think there will be any problem, but if there is, give me a call." He closed his medical bag and left Mr. Swift, Rick, and Tom in the lab.

"We're going to have to go to the police with this, Tom," Mr. Swift said. "I don't know who these people think they are, but they kidnapped you and Rick, and we can't let them get away with it."

"Wait, Dad. Don't call in Chief Montague. Rick and I broke into Loew Industries, after all." Tom sat up, his head hurting. More and more, his memory was returning, but with it came waves of pain.

"That hardly matters. They gave you some drug," an angry Mr. Swift said. "Who knows what you might have done?"

"Yeah, you were so out of it you fell over the wall," Rick pointed out.

"If you're sure this Dr. Loew is responsible for the dumping," Mr. Swift continued, "the police *must* be brought in. And we have to inform the EPA."

Tom's mind raced. He remembered something else—his portable analyzer and the waste water samples from Loew Industries.

"Rick, would you do me a favor?" Tom asked. "Check the van and see if those water samples are there."

"Will do." Rick gave Tom a grin and a small salute, then jogged out of the lab.

In five minutes he was back, his expression now serious. "Guess what?" he said. "The samples are gone."

Tom sighed. "Why am I not surprised?" He turned to his father. "Without any evidence we can't go to the EPA. And it'll take them a couple of days to get a team out. By then Loew could have stopped the dumping. He knows we're onto him."

"Still, Tom, I have to inform them."

"Go on," Tom said, "but we have to keep after Dr. Loew and get real evidence. We have to *prove* to the EPA that the contaminated water came from his plant."

"I'm going to tell Chief Montague about this," Mr. Swift insisted. He checked his watch. "But not in the middle of the night. I'll call her first thing in the morning and ask her to come out."

"All right," Tom said. "I'm going to rest here awhile. Rick can get me home."

Mr. Swift shrugged. "Okay. I'll see you back home, then," he said, and left.

Tom sank back in his chair and swung around to face his friend. "What went on at Loew Industries that I don't know about?" Tom asked. "I remember some, but not everything." Tom straightened. "The girl. I've seen her someplace before."

"That was Dr. Loew's daughter."

Tom felt as if a bombshell had exploded in his head. With that revelation came a flood of memories.

"Are you sure?" Tom swallowed hard.

"I overheard her talking with the two goons who were going to experiment on me. She was responsible for getting me out," Rick said. He quickly told Tom everything that had happened to him. Finishing, Rick said, "She looked worried and said she might have been wrong about you."

"She's been following me. She was the girl at the beach party, the one who punctured the van tire—and the one who took the pictures of me taking samples at Laguna Pequeña. She told me her name is Melanie. So she's Dr. Loew's daughter, huh? I can't believe she's involved in dumping the hGh."

"But why is her father doing it? He's a weird dude, but still . . ." Rick said.

"Put it all together, Rick. Loew is conducting illegal experiments with genetically engineered human growth hormone. He's been dumping the residue into the ocean, and now he's trying to lay the blame on Swift Enterprises. But that's not the worst of it," Tom said grimly.

"That's bad enough. That and wanting his two goons to experiment on *me*." Rick shivered at the memory.

"From what you said, he's probably been experimenting on himself. We don't know much about Loew. I'd never heard of him before tonight, but he's obviously a brilliant researcher."

"So if he's using his gunk on himself, why is he so short?" Rick asked.

"What if he was shorter before he started?" Tom countered. *"Much shorter?"*

"You mean a dwarf?" Rick shook his head. "Your brain's still cobwebby from the stuff they gave you, Tom."

"I don't think so. He had dozens of books on endocrinology in his office. Lack of a human growth hormone called somatotropin might have stunted his growth—and he could have learned how to overcome the deficiency."

"There's no telling what he might be doing to himself. He lost it totally when he was talking to his two goons," Rick said.

Tom nodded, then yawned. The effects of the drug were wearing off, leaving him so tired he could hardly keep his eyes open.

"Time to get you home. And this time I'll drive," Rick said, as they headed for the parking lot.

"You won't hear any argument from me," Tom mumbled. "And, Rick?"

"Yeah?"

"Thanks. I appreciate all you've done tonight," Tom said. "I owe you for this."

"You better believe it!" Rick laughed.

They got into Tom's van and roared off into

the night. A short while later they arrived at the Swift family home. Rick transferred to his own car, and Tom went inside. He was asleep seconds after his head hit the pillow.

But Tom came awake when he heard someone moving in his room. He sat up, then gasped. A huge misshapen shadow towered above him.

Tom pushed himself to his feet and turned on the light. Standing at the foot of his bed was Rob. The seven-foot-tall robot had come between the wall and the window and had cast the unusual—and unexpected—shadow that had spooked Tom.

"You startled me," Tom said, heaving a sigh of relief. "What are you doing here?"

"I came to alert you to our results."

Tom dropped to the bed and calmed down before asking, "What do you want to tell me? This better be good"—he glanced at the clock on his nightstand—"I've had only about three hours of sleep."

"The hGh-eating bacteria project has been successful, Tom," Rob solemnly intoned.

"Excellent!" Tom shot to his feet, forgetting all about his fatigue. He was running on adrenaline now. He threw on his clothes, saying, "Tell me all about it."

"Orb has a complete report. Do you wish me to accept a telecommunications relay on it?" Rob asked. The tall robot had built-in remote capability for communicating with Orb.

"No, I want to check it myself." Tom stopped in the hall, scribbled a quick note to his parents, and then left with Rob for the Hydro-Projects Wing lab and his experiment.

The lab was quiet when he entered. Orb sat on the counter next to the nutrient tanks, clicking and humming with power. Tom pulled up a chair and sat in front of his computer console, where he punched in his request for full information.

"That's it!" he cried after looking over the results. "We've done it. We can release our new bacteria, and they'll completely devour Loew's spilled hGh."

"So it appears, Tom," Orb said. "The computer simulation agrees with our limited testing."

"You're telling me to be one hundred percent sure before I do anything, aren't you?"

"That is a more prudent course than telling everyone you have the problem solved. There might be unforeseen elements we have not properly studied." Orb waited for Tom's reply.

"We can do a small trial run down at Laguna Pequeña," Tom said, thinking hard. "Prepare a test tube with the bioengineered bacteria in a nutrient solution," Tom ordered. He started a computer check to go through hundreds of thousands of possible problems to see if anything turned up. But he knew that the tests he ran at Laguna Pequeña would matter most. Everything else was just simulation.

"All done, Tom," Rob said. "Do you wish us to accompany you?"

"No need," Tom said, glancing at the clock. It was after seven, and he wanted to start right away. Rob and Orb always attracted attention. This time Tom wanted to work as quietly as possible.

"We will continue attempts to perfect the bacteria," Orb said. "Megatron suggests several minor gene alterations."

"I'll go test it, then meet you and Rob back here with my results," Tom promised. He packed the glass tube in a special case and left the lab. He drove his van to the beach and found a spot near the discharge pipes that would be good for his tests.

Tom took samples of the water, labeled them, and then released his hGh-hungry bacteria into the sea. He took new samples every two minutes, and at the end of ten minutes poured a special solution into the water that would instantly kill his bacteria.

After carefully packing away his samples, Tom climbed into his van and drove back to the Hydro-Projects Wing. He was anxious to see if his newly created bacteria had eaten the hGh as well as the projections had promised.

"Here, Rob," Tom said, handing the case to Rob. "Check the samples to see how efficient our man-made microorganism was."

"Right away, Tom," Rob said. "Orb predicts complete success."

"I've got my fingers crossed that you're right," Tom said, setting down in front of his computer.

"We would also," Orb piped up, "but we lack sufficient digital dexterity for that."

Tom laughed. He kept working for several hours. When his telephone rang, he punched the button on his console to answer.

"Hello?"

There was silence for a moment, then a soft voice said, "Tom? Tom Swift?"

"Yes, who is this?"

"It's me. Melanie Loew." She began sobbing.

"What's wrong?' Tom asked.

"I can't talk on the phone," she said tearfully.

"Let's meet," Tom suggested, wondering what was going on.

"At the beach. Where we met last time," she said.

"When?"

Tom waited for Melanie's answer, but all he heard was a click as the line went dead.

11

TOM SAT IN HIS LAB AND TRIED TO FIGURE OUT
what to do. Melanie had called in distress and
had been cut off. Or had she hung up rather
than be overheard?

"Her father might have caught her," Tom
muttered. No matter why the line had gone
dead, things didn't look good for the girl.

Tom figured that Melanie Loew was the key
to clearing everything up. She could provide
the answers Tom needed to clear Swift Enterprises—and himself—of all charges of illegal
dumping of active genetic material. And then
he thought about what Dr. Loew had tried to
do to Rick.

Tom shuddered at the idea of using human

105

subjects for any experiment in growth hormone research. He knew Rick had been lucky—and that Dr. Loew exhibited signs of hGh gone wild.

The uncontrolled dumping, the mutated sea creatures, all the result of this man carrying on illegal experiments—and probably on himself, Tom mused. The man had to be stopped, but Tom worried that he still didn't have the solid proof he needed. Bottles of contaminated ocean water wouldn't be enough. He needed more, especially since Mitch Carlton had shown Melanie's photographs on TV.

But Melanie might be in real trouble. Tom made a decision. He shook himself alert and quickly left the Hydro-Projects Wing. He got in his van and drove to Laguna Pequeña. In the parking lot at the beach he saw Melanie's car and pulled the van into a space opposite it. Tom got out and looked up and down the beach. He saw a figure huddled on the sand just beyond the reach of the incoming waves.

"Melanie!" he called, but she gave no sign of recognition. Tom headed toward her.

"Melanie," he called again. "Are you all right?" When he was less than ten feet away, he saw that she was sobbing quietly.

Tom walked over to her and touched her on the shoulder. She started, then turned toward him.

"Thank you for coming, Tom. I was so wrong about you. I'm sorry, I'm so sorry!" She began crying openly now. She pulled her knees up higher and hugged them tight.

"What's wrong? I'm trying to figure out this dumping business and think I know most of it, but I need your help." Tom sat beside the girl. He couldn't help thinking that the surfing would have been great that day—if Laguna Pequeña weren't closed.

"He told me you were responsible for discharging the growth hormone into the water," Melanie said. "He said you were corrupt and would do anything to discredit him. When I called you he made me hang up."

"You mean Dr. Loew? Your dad?"

Melanie looked at him with tear-filled eyes and nodded. "He told me you and your father were wicked and hated him because he was a dwarf."

"I'd never even heard of your father before last night. And I don't think my dad had heard of him, either," Tom said, surprised at Melanie's admission.

"That doesn't matter to him. He—he's gotten it into his head that anyone more successful has to be getting special favors." Melanie took in a deep breath. "And he resents everyone who's taller than he is."

Tom felt sorry for Lawrence Loew and

107

angry that the scientist had involved his daughter in his mad schemes.

"He's experimenting with growth hormone, then dumping the waste products. *He* is the one responsible for those hideous things out there." Melanie pointed across the choppy water. "He's doing it to discredit you."

"Why? What have we ever done to him to make him want to ruin Swift Enterprises?" Tom was genuinely puzzled.

"I don't know. Maybe nothing. He's changed so much since he began his experiment. He thinks everyone is against him."

"He's using the hGh on himself, isn't he?" Tom said as gently as he could. "That's dangerous because of the ways it can affect his mind. His body might grow, but the hGh causes neurotransmitter imbalances in the brain."

"I don't know about these things," Melanie said, standing up and brushing herself off. "All I know is that he's grown almost a foot taller, but he's so different."

A sudden thought hit Tom and sent him scrambling to his feet. "He sent your pictures of me to Carlton, didn't he?"

Melanie bit her lower lip and nodded.

"They were incriminating because they seemed to show you secretly pouring some strange liquid into the water."

Tom felt a rush of relief pour over him. Melanie hadn't tried to frame him, after all.

"I knew you were taking samples, not dumping the hGh," she said. "But Daddy didn't care." Melanie swallowed hard. "He flies into violent rages these days and thinks everyone is out to steal his formula."

"He hasn't harmed you, has he?" Tom asked.

Melanie shook her head. "No, never. I'm the only one who can control him now. Carter and Lundquist, his two assistants, can't even talk to him. Last night was the worst it's ever been."

"Are they the two who drugged me?" Tom asked.

"Drugged you? I told them to make sure you got home. What did they do?" From Melanie's expression, Tom knew she was truly upset.

Tom quickly explained what had happened. By the time he finished, Melanie was crying again.

"This is awful! I believed my father when he said you were corrupt and out to ruin him. And I thought he was doing a public service when he phoned in that anonymous tip to the television reporter."

"He's your father, and you love him," Tom said. He reached out to her, but she jerked away and rushed forward into the surf, crying as she ran. Tom raced after her.

Melanie dived into the water and thrashed around, fighting against him. "Leave me alone. Let me go!"

"You'll hurt yourself," Tom protested, swimming around to get a lifeguard's grip on her. "Come back to shore."

Ducking, Melanie evaded Tom's grasp and swam farther out. He sucked in a lungful of air and stroked powerfully after her.

Then she vanished.

Tom treaded water and looked around. Melanie was nowhere to be seen.

"Melanie! Where are you?" Tom's heart raced. These were dangerous waters, thanks to the mutant monsters her father had spawned.

Then, as Tom scanned the surface of the ocean, a snaky orange tentacle covered with huge, pulsating suckers thrust itself up from the water in front of him.

For a moment Tom froze. Then he dived— only to feel another massive tentacle closing around his middle.

Tom fought to get back to the surface, but the monstrous suckers exerted their cruel effect. He could feel chunks of skin coming loose as the suckers raked over him. Clawing frantically, he managed to pry free the powerful tentacle and shoot to the surface, gasping for air.

Spinning in the water, he got a quick glimpse of Melanie hanging limp in one of the giant monster's other tentacles. The mutant beast was coiled around her and squeezing hard.

Tom shook the water out of his eyes. This had to be the same creature that had attacked Mandy—only it had mutated even more!

It looked a little like a squid, but only because of the tentacles. No squid Tom had ever seen was orange with pulsing gray veins on its head. And the eyes! They bulged with unbridled fury! Then the beast disappeared underwater with Melanie in its grip.

"Melanie, hang on!" Tom shouted, getting ready to dive. At that moment the squid shot back up from beneath Tom. He was tossed around, clawing wildly at the slimy flesh. A tentacle circled his body again. Tom screamed when he looked up into the monster's gaping mouth.

Six-inch-long fangs snapped at him!

Tom narrowly avoided the savage slashing attack. From the corner of his eye, he saw that Melanie was struggling weakly in the hideous mutation's tentacles.

Tom let out a cry of pure rage at the beast. He kicked and punched, landing one blow just under the squid's eye. As it jerked its spine-topped head back and bellowed in pain, Tom saw the only chance for him and Melanie to escape.

He pummeled the squid's eye with punch after punch. A sluggish flow of blood began to ooze from the cut he had opened—and the beast reacted to the pain as Tom had hoped.

Its tentacles relaxed, releasing Tom and Melanie. Then it dived for the safety of the ocean bottom. They were free!

Swimming over to Melanie, Tom asked, "Are you all right?" She moaned and muttered something he didn't understand. Reassured that she was still alive, Tom put one arm around her and swam hard for the beach.

"Melanie?" he said. The girl lay on the sand, unmoving. Her eyelids fluttered, but she didn't come to.

Tom picked Melanie up and carried her to his van. He considered his next move. The Hydro-Projects Wing was nearby. Melanie didn't seem to be seriously injured, but she needed attention. Tom used the cellular phone in his van to call home.

Sandra answered.

Tom quickly explained what had happened. "I need to talk to Dad," he said.

"He's gone already," Sandra told him. "He's meeting with Chief Montague about what happened to you at Loew Industries, and then he was going to give a briefing to the EPA scientists."

"I can't call Melanie's father—he's the one who's responsible for all this," Tom said.

"Take her the Hydro-Projects Wing," Sandra said. "We'll join you there."

"We? I thought you said Dad was gone."

"Mandy will be here in a couple of minutes. We were going up to Playa Bonita to check it out."

"Fill a dry-ice locker with some nu-skin," Tom said, referring to his miraculous skin replacement invention. Both he and Melanie would need it to treat the places on their bodies where the creature's suckers had ripped away patches of skin. "We can let Melanie rest on the cot in the storeroom," Tom said. "Then call Dr. Yukawa and get him out to the new lab. See you there in half an hour." He hung up the phone and looked into the rear of the van at Melanie. She was lying quietly on a blanket he had tossed on the floor.

Tom knew he ought to take her to a hospital, but he feared what might happen if her father was notified and came to claim her.

Tom had just started the van when a car passed behind him. He watched in the rearview mirror as two men parked and got out. It took Tom a few seconds to recognize them. They were taller than he remembered, but these were Carter and Lundquist, Dr. Loew's two assistants. They went to Melanie's car and peered inside.

Tom backed out of the parking lot and drove off slowly, hoping they wouldn't notice him. But they did. The men ran for their car.

Tom floored the accelerator, making sure the van's safety system was working.

The car screeched as it made a tight U-turn right behind him.

"If you want to race," Tom said, setting his jaw, "let's do it!"

12

TOM SWUNG AROUND A CORNER AND FELT THE van's computer guidance system correct spinout of the rear wheels. Settling down, he took the turns in the road expertly, but the car with Dr. Loew's two assistants kept pace. Tom glanced over his shoulder and saw Melanie rolling from side to side in the rear of the van. If the chase went on for long, there was a good chance she'd get hurt smashing into the side panels.

Tom guided the van onto the road leading to the gate not far from the Hydro-Projects Wing. In the rearview mirror he saw the car tailing him go into a skid. The driver fought to keep control, and then Tom lost sight of the car in a rising cloud of dust.

He smiled, certain he could get inside the fence surrounding the Hydro-Projects Wing before Carter and Lundquist could catch him. He just had to make sure he had enough of a lead so that the gate could close before Loew's men reached it.

Tom accelerated toward it, knowing that the remote sensor in his van was sending a recognition signal.

In an instant the gate automatically slid open. The van blasted through the opening, and the gate immediately closed behind it. He heaved a sigh of relief. Safe! Security would take care of Carter and Lundquist if they tried to follow.

Tom took only a minute or two to pull into the parking lot outside the new lab. He was surprised to find Sandra and Mandy waiting for him. He opened the side door of the van and picked up Melanie. The girl moaned and stirred, then put her arms around his neck and began sobbing.

"You two look like drowned rats," Mandy said. "What happened?"

"I'll give you all the gory details when we get Melanie into the building." Tom carried Melanie up the steps and into the lobby. "By the way, two of Melanie's father's assistants are hot on my heels."

"So what happened, Tom? Come on, give." Mandy was insistent.

"First aid, then answers," he said. With Mandy trailing him, Tom headed straight for the storeroom where Sandra had already prepared the cot. Gently Tom lowered Melanie onto it. Then he opened the dry-ice locker that Sandra had brought and expertly began applying layers of nu-skin to the areas of flesh burned by the mutated monster's acid touch. When he finished, Tom applied nu-skin to his own burns. The instant it touched his skin, he felt the soothing, healing ointment it was soaked in begin to work. He then bandaged the spots where he had applied his wondrous invention.

"Dr. Yukawa is on his way, and I tried to phone Harlan Ames to tell him about the guys who were after you," Sandra said, coming into the room. "Harlan didn't answer, so I left a message."

"We really need to contact him," Tom said. Now that the adrenaline had stopped pumping through his body, he realized that a fence wouldn't stop Loew's assistants if they wanted to get inside badly enough.

"What's wrong, Tom? You look worried," Mandy said. "Can they get to us?"

Tom motioned for Mandy and Sandra to leave Melanie to rest and follow him out of the storeroom. "We're safe enough in here," Tom replied when they were back in the lobby. "I caught sight of them for only a few seconds, but there was something odd about them."

"Sure there was," Sandra retorted. "They're weird enough to work for a monster."

"Melanie confirmed what I suspected," Tom told the girls. "Loew is taking his own experimental growth hormone, and it's made him totally paranoid. That's why he's so sure we're out to get him. The bioengineered hGh has side effects he either dismissed or was willing to risk. Also, he might have developed a brain tumor. Taking the growth hormone is similar to hypersecretion, which can cause cancer." Tom looked through the front doors toward the distant gate, hoping not to see Loew's two assistants. So far, so good.

"So the hGh caused the changes in Loew's body?" Sandra asked.

"Yes, and personality changes as well," Tom said, leading the girls into his lab. "Melanie confirmed that his appearance is changing radically."

"Too much growth hormone?" Mandy asked. She swallowed hard.

"Exactly. He's exchanging added height for mental problems and acromegaly—giantism." Tom paced back and forth. "What's keeping Dr. Yukawa? I don't think anything is seriously wrong with Melanie, but I want to be sure."

"I showed Mandy how well George is doing," Sandra said. "He's perfectly healthy. No tumors or anything else out of the ordinary. What might have gone wrong with Loew's formula?"

"I can't be sure. I managed to identify Loew's growth hormone, but there are one hundred ninety-one amino acids in the polypeptide chain. How many different ways can that go wrong?" Tom went to the phone and picked it up.

"Don't be so impatient, Tom," Sandra chided. "Dr. Yukawa will be here soon."

"It's Harlan I'm wondering about. He ought to have called to report on perimeter security. I don't want those two goons waltzing in." Tom dialed the Swift Enterprises security chief and waited as the phone rang and rang. Just as he was about to try a different number, Harlan Ames answered.

"What is it?" the man asked gruffly.

In the background Tom could hear angry shouts. "Harlan, what's happening?" he asked.

"Sorry, Tom, but things are buzzing here. The latest demonstration is turning ugly."

"I thought that stuff had all stopped," Tom said.

"They've been coming back since the judge refused Carlton's request to shut down Swift Enterprises. Wait a second, Tom." Tom heard sounds of a scuffle. Then Harlan Ames came back on the line.

"Two demonstrators just tried to scale the fence," he reported. "We have them in custody, but the others are threatening to rush the main gate. We called the police, but they haven't arrived yet. So what did you want?"

"Two of Loew's men chased me to the new wing," Tom told him, "but I lost them outside the fence. I wanted to be sure they stayed there."

"I'll check when I can, Tom," Harlan promised, "but as wild as this crowd is getting, it might be a while."

Tom hung up and told his sister and Mandy what was happening. Then he sat down at his computer and tapped into Megatron's security system. The massive computer buried under the administration building at Swift Enterprises controlled most facets of activity within the complex and was remotely linked with the new wing. Everything from sprinklers to vacuum cleaners to perimeter sensors ran through Megatron.

"Wow, look at this!" Tom exclaimed, pointing to the computer screen. Mandy and Sandra crowded behind him. A perimeter map of the Hydro-Projects Wing was displayed, and two red points flashed on it.

"What is it, Tom?" Sandra asked anxiously.

"Those points must be Carter and Lundquist. Somehow they got over the fence and are coming straight here." Tom was concerned—the Hydro-Projects Wing wasn't designed to be a fortress.

"We should call the police," Mandy said, a slight quaver in her voice.

"Harlan has done that already," Tom pointed out. "They'll clean up the problems at the main gate before coming over."

"You mean we have to deal with those two goons by ourselves?" Mandy asked. "How do you suggest we do that?"

"Don't worry," Tom said, typing instructions into the computer. "I've just sealed all doors into the Hydro-Projects Wing."

"But they can break the windows," Mandy protested.

Tom laughed and shook his head. "The windows look like glass, but they aren't. They're made of a special transparent plastic designed for deep ocean probes."

"It can withstand any pounding those guys can deliver," Sandra added.

"They're almost here," Tom said, watching

Carter and Lundquist's progress on his computer screen. "They'll be coming up the steps now, and yes, there they are at the front door."

Tom leaned back in his chair and heard the two men banging on the door. He thought of the wolf huffing and puffing at the Three Little Pigs' houses. These wolves would never blow down his high-tech plastic walls.

"Tom," Mandy said uneasily, "are you sure they can't get in?"

"It would take someone with the strength of Rob to punch through those panels," Tom assured her. But a horrible, metallic grinding sound sent them rushing to the lobby. There, on the other side of the door, were Carter and Lundquist.

Back at the beach Tom had noticed that something about them had looked strange. Now he saw what it was. Their pants were too short, and their shirts strained to cover massive muscles.

"Sandra, Mandy, get to the storeroom and stay there with Melanie!" Tom cried. "They're breaking the metal supports holding the plastic panels!"

"How can they possibly be strong enough to do that?" Sandra asked as she and Mandy backed away.

"The growth hormone!" Tom declared.

"That has to be it. Dr. Loew has experimented on his own assistants. Now get going."

As he spoke, a large panel of heavy plastic crashed flat onto the lobby floor, and the two men burst in.

"Where's Melanie?" one of Loew's assistants asked in a rasping voice.

Tom recognized the hoarseness as a side effect of too much hGh. From the name tag on the man's shirt, Tom identified him as Carter. "This way," Tom said. He inched backward toward his lab, his mind racing. He remembered his previous encounter with these two. They had overpowered him even before the growth hormone had given them bulging muscles. He needed to put them out of commission fast, before they could do any damage to the labs—or to him.

"Dr. Loew fed you his formula, didn't he?" Tom asked, playing for time. "It works fast to have bulked you guys up in less than a day."

"Where is Melanie? Dr. Loew ordered us to return her to the laboratory," said the other assistant, Lundquist. The two men lunged awkwardly at Tom. He jumped backward so that he was flat against the closed door to his lab.

As the two mutated men reached for him

Tom opened the lab door and shouted, "They want to hurt me, Rob. Stop them!"

"Yes, Tom." The towering silver robot moved to intercept the two men who seemed unfazed by Rob's appearance.

Tom ducked as Carter made a grab for him. A meaty fist more like a bucket of knuckles swung past his head and crashed into the doorframe. Tom noticed that Carter showed no sign of pain. The man's neural receptors were beginning to burn out, Tom realized. In this condition, pain wouldn't stop him, broken bones wouldn't stop him, perhaps even a steel-jacketed seven-foot robot wouldn't stop him.

"Rob!" Tom yelled. The huge robot moved with incredible speed to knock aside a second blow that might have killed Tom. Tom dashed into the lab and scooped up a high-power cutting laser from the workbench but hesitated to use it. The laser could cut through a foot of steel in seconds, and he didn't want to kill either Carter or Lundquist.

Taking the laser, Tom managed to scramble around the melee and roll out of the lab. He slammed the reinforced door behind him, hoping that Rob would be able to keep Carter and Lundquist inside. But Carter's strength was immense. Moments later Tom heard something being slammed against the door from the inside. Then again and again, each time with more force. Tom watched in disbelief as cracks appeared in the door, and then it shattered with a horrible splitting sound. The force of the door exploding outward knocked Tom down amid a shower of wood and metal splinters.

Tom howled in pain and looked down to see a four-inch piece of jagged wood sticking out of his thigh.

Rob reacted immediately to Tom's scream. He zoomed away from Lundquist and helped Tom up. "Don't worry about me, Rob," Tom said. "We have to find a way to stop those guys!"

"Get to safety, Tom. I'll try to disable them without causing significant damage." Rob placed himself in the shattered lab doorway as Tom limped his way down the hall.

Tom opened the next door he came to, the tank room. He looked back before going inside, though, and was astonished at what he saw. Together Carter and Lundquist ran at Rob and knocked the gleaming robot to the floor.

Tom backed into the tank room as Carter picked himself up and began stumbling down the hall in Tom's direction. Lundquist tried to rise, but Rob grabbed his ankle in a steely grip.

Tom began to close the door to the tank room, but Carter moved faster than Tom had thought possible. The door swung back open with incredible force, knocking Tom down. The cutting laser went flying from his hand, skidding to a stop beneath the huge standing tank that held George and his cousins.

"I can only hold this one, Tom. Please attend to the other," Rob called from down the hall.

Tom swallowed hard. Waves of pain from the wood in his thigh washed over him, and his vision began to cloud.

Can't pass out now, he told himself. Gritting his teeth against the pain, Tom reached down and pulled the jagged fragment from his thigh. Then he quickly stripped off his T-shirt and tied it around his leg above the wound.

Carter growled deep in his throat and hoisted a workbench above his head. Tom knew that the bench weighed a good five hundred pounds.

Still on the floor, Tom pushed himself backward with his hands, Carter's burning eyes fixed on him. Carter advanced slowly, backing Tom up against a tank. There was nowhere for Tom to go—he was caught like a fish on a line.

13

CARTER STAGGERED CLOSER, HEAVING THE workbench high over his head to throw it at Tom. Instinctively Tom tried to move away—and his hand bumped against a familiar object. The cutting laser! Tom grabbed it off the floor and raised it in one quick motion. Seeing this, Carter shouted in rage.

Tom fired—but not at the man. The laser burned a hole in the giant fish tank behind Carter. A thick stream of water shot from the tank as though from a fire hose.

Carter stumbled, the weight of the workbench throwing him backward. The bench crashed into the fish tank, shattering the glass already weakened by the laser hole. A torrent of water rushed out. Carter fought and lost his balance. He crashed heavily to the floor, amid wiggling fish and broken glass. Tom struggled to his feet and limped toward the door. He looked down at the hulking figure beginning to rise from the floor. Carter was bleeding from a hundred cuts—pieces of glass stuck out of his body in a dozen places—but he seemed not to notice. Reaching the doorway, Tom looked down the hall. There was Rob, squeezing Lundquist in a bear hug and carrying the kicking, flailing man toward Tom.

"I see you managed to get the other one down," Rob said as he stopped at the tank room doorway.

"Yes," Tom said, "but I don't think he'll stay that way."

"If I relax my hold, I'm afraid this one will get loose," Rob said. Lundquist was smashing his fist into Rob with such force that Tom could see dents in Rob's tough exterior.

Tom thought fast and said, "Pressure point, Rob! The carotid artery—without blood in his brain, he'll lose consciousness, no matter how strong he is."

Rob moved one hand to Lundquist's neck with lightning speed. The hormone-filled giant began to struggle free, then slumped down. Rob released his hold, and Lundquist crashed to the floor—just as Carter rose to his feet. The man was a nightmare vision of bulging eyes and dripping blood. Rob reached out to stop him, but Carter tumbled to the floor again, loss of blood finally sapping him of his superhuman strength.

Tom heard footsteps coming down the hall. He spun, fearing more of Dr. Loew's men, then slumped in relief when he saw three police officers. Behind them in the lobby he saw Chief Robin Montague speaking with Sandra and Mandy.

"Handcuff them," Tom said, pointing to Carter and Lundquist, "but be very careful. When they wake up, they'll be a lot stronger than you could imagine."

Chief Montague came into the tank room, almost slipping in the water.

"Excuse me a second, Chief," Tom said, hurrying to rescue a huge bass. "Rob! Help me get this guy into another tank." Tom tried to lift the giant fish, but it was too heavy.

"Right away, Tom," Rob answered. The robot gently lifted the bass and dropped it into another tank with a loud splash. Then Rob did the same with the other fish.

Tom heaved a sigh of relief when the last of the experimental fish were safely deposited in other tanks. He turned up the oxygen levels to keep them going until he could transfer them to a new tank of their own.

"I'm glad you got here when you did," Tom said, turning back to Chief Montague. "Things were getting tense."

"And fishy," Chief Montague said. "As soon as we arrived at the demonstration, Harlan Ames hustled us straight out here." She looked around the tank room. "Your father told us how you got shot up with a drug at Loew Industries. And Rick—"

"Tom!" Mandy cried, bursting in and interrupting the chief. "You're hurt!"

From behind her Sandra said, "I'll get the first-aid kit," and ran down the hall.

"The bleeding's stopped," Tom said, looking down at the red-stained T-shirt tied around his leg. "The cut just needs to be cleaned and dressed."

As he was talking, Mandy found an undamaged chair in the room and brought it over for Tom to sit on. "Thanks, Mandy," Tom said, flashing her a smile. To Chief Montague he said, "Loew wasn't the one who drugged me. It was the two creeps your men are hauling out now."

Tom turned toward the door and pointed. There was Melanie standing beside Sandra, a first-aid kit in hand, her face pale. She came in, made a large cut in Tom's jeans, and began to clean the wound in his leg.

"Chief, there's more," Melanie said as she worked. "My father is Lawrence Loew, and he's responsible for releasing—"

Tom grabbed Melanie by the arm and whispered in her ear. She stopped and shook her head.

"Chief Montague, let me talk with Melanie a second," Tom said. Melanie finished tying the bandage and helped Tom to stand. He smiled and said, "Thanks." Then he walked her over to one side of the room and spoke urgently. "The chief will have to arrest your father if you tell her everything."

"But I've got to!" Melanie protested. "My father's not responsible for his actions any longer. Look at the damage he's done to Laguna Pequeña's marine life. He's lied to me. And he hasn't treated you and Rick too well, either."

"I'm glad you feel that way," said Tom. "Right now he's out of control. He's got to be stopped from using his artificial growth hormone before he causes any more damage."

"I know. Not only did my father inject Carter and Lundquist with his new hGh, he's about to experiment on others," Melanie admitted. There was an edge of terror in her voice.

"We can stop him, and I think I can reverse the damage he's already done. He should never have taken the growth hormone," Tom continued. "It clearly made him do things he never would have considered before. I want to talk to him before the police do and get his help in cleaning up Laguna Pequeña.

"What do you want me to do, Tom?" Melanie asked.

"Stay with Sandra and Mandy. I need to look over the results of the tests Rob and Orb were running. If my hGh-eating microbe is as effective as I think, I can clean up the genetic material that's been dumped into the ocean."

"What about my father?"

"I think we can work with the authorities to see that he gets the attention he needs before he's locked up."

"And the damage?" Melanie said. "What about that?"

"He'll have to make full restitution, but I don't believe any permanent damage has been done to the coastal ecology."

"What's going on?" Chief Montague demanded. "I have to get back to talk to the media. Do you have anything more for me?"

"Go ahead, Chief. We might need to talk with you later, but I don't think so." Tom looked at Melanie, who smiled weakly.

"Come down to the station soon, Tom, and

press formal charges against those two goons," the chief said. She left, shaking her head.

"This is dangerous, Tom," said Sandra. "You should have told Chief Montague about Dr. Loew."

"What purpose would that have served? Besides, I think I can undo all the damage he's done."

"Can you reverse the contamination along Laguna Pequeña?" asked Mandy. "That seems like a major cleanup job."

"I've identified the specific DNA being dumped. Rob and Orb have been working on a special new strain of bacteria that will eat only the polypeptide chain released by Dr. Loew."

"Tom—" Melanie started to say.

"It'll be all right. Mandy and Sandra will look after you. I need to finish looking over the results on how my bioengineered bacteria reacted in a saltwater environment."

Sandra and Melanie left, but Mandy hung back. She smiled at Tom and said, "This is really very nice of you, not having Melanie's father arrested. Do you think he'll agree to help fix all the damage he's done?"

"I hope it works out," Tom said.

"It will. I have confidence in you," Mandy said. She took a step toward Tom and gave him a quick kiss, just as Sandra yelled for her to come on. Mandy smiled and said, "See you later."

Tom watched Mandy leave, then heaved a sigh. The tank room was a mess, his lab was a mess, and he had so much to do. The fight with Carter and Lundquist had been a hint of what Loew's growth hormone could do in a short time.

Dr. Loew had been taking it for days, maybe weeks or even months. Tom had to be ready for him. He went back to his lab, ignoring the mess, and began to rummage through cabinet drawers and pull electronics parts from storage bins.

"It's a good thing I showed up," Rick said several hours later. "You're taking a mighty big risk. This is something the authorities ought to handle."

"The authorities like Mitch Carlton?" Tom shot back.

"He's still making a big splash on the news at your expense," Rick admitted. "But your dad is meeting with the EPA officials now, and he said Swift Enterprises is in the clear. When the judge didn't issue the restraining order, it was just the start of good things going your way."

"That makes it all the more urgent for us

to get to Dr. Loew. Carlton and the press will be looking for someone to take the blame. He won't want to admit he was wrong about Swift Enterprises."

"But Loew *is* guilty!" Rick protested.

"I know, but the authorities will go easier on him if he acknowledges how dangerous the dumping was and makes an effort to correct the damage," Tom said. Getting through to Loew was going to take the tact of a diplomat.

"I know you feel sorry for Melanie," Rick said, "but I don't have a soft spot in my heart—or in my head—for Dr. Loew. Not after he told his goons to experiment on me." Rick looked at the suit Tom was now holding up. "What is that, anyway?"

"It's something I cobbled together to protect myself from Dr. Loew," Tom explained. "It's made in layers. I can charge up the outer layer and be insulated by the inner one."

"So you become a human shocking machine," Rick said. "So what?"

"Loew might be as strong as his two assistants by now," Tom said. "I made the mistake of taking on Carter and Lundquist with my bare hands. Loew won't be able to touch me once this is charged."

"Take Rob," Rick suggested. The huge

robot continued working on the hGh-eating bacteria and didn't look up.

"Rob has to stay here to finish his work with Orb and clean up," Tom explained. "I think if I can talk to Loew one-on-one, there's a better chance he'll listen."

"Tom," Rick said seriously, "he'll still go to prison."

"Probably, but he needs medical help first, and his sentence won't be as long if he cooperates fully before the police and the EPA get there." Tom held up four small devices. Two were the size of shirt buttons, and the others looked like small rubber earplugs.

"The buttons are transmitters," Tom told Rick.

"I get it," Rick said. "And the other gizmos are receivers." Rick took one and stuck it in his ear. "I guess you want me to stay outside and wait for a signal, while you go in." He started to protest, but Tom cut him off.

"I won't be in any danger as long as I'm wearing the electrosuit and you're waiting for my signal." Tom fastened the transmitter under his collar where he could activate it easily, and Rick did the same. "Well?"

"All right, Tom. Let's go. You want me to follow you out?"

"That might be best," Tom said. "I'll give

Rob and Orb their instructions for spraying the hGh-eating bacteria into the water."

"The place looks deserted," Rick observed. Loew Industries might have been abandoned for all the signs of life within its high wire fence.

"It does," Tom agreed. "The main gate is open, and it looks as if that door is, too." He pointed to a front door that stood ajar.

"Tom, let me go in with you. This is too weird."

"Thanks, Rick, but I'll be okay." Tom put on his shiny, loose-fitting electrosuit. Then he attached leads to a battery in the rear of the van.

"Stand back, Rick, while I charge."

"This will never catch on," Rick said, smiling crookedly. "But then, you never did have any fashion sense."

"Don't touch!" Tom warned when Rick reached out. "The electrified strips along my arms, legs, and body will give you one humongous shock." The suit crackled with electricity as sparks danced up and down the silvery sleeves and pant legs.

"You're running the show," Rick said, throwing up his hands. He turned and got back into his Jaguar.

Tom walked onto the grounds of Loew Industries, being careful not to touch any metal that might discharge the electricity in his suit. He entered the building and walked slowly down the corridors, listening intently for any sound. He heard nothing. Tom paused outside a door marked with Dr. Loew's name. Hesitantly he looked inside the scientist's office. Loew wasn't there.

Shuffling down the deserted corridors in his electrosuit, Tom listened hard. His pulse raced when he heard glassware clinking. He stopped and looked through the door into a lab. For a moment he didn't recognize the man inside.

Dr. Loew had changed radically. He was taller than Tom now, easily six feet six. But the changes hadn't stopped with height. He had lost all of his hair, and his flesh had the look of yellowed parchment. Veins throbbed visibly just under the skin.

The most striking change Tom noticed was in Dr. Loew's body contours. All his body fat had been burned up by the growth hormone, and his muscles rippled like a body builder's. Aside from the unmistakable broad face, Dr. Loew looked nothing like his former self.

The man moved nervously from one part of the lab to another, talking aloud to himself as he went. Tom noticed that Loew ate constantly, the caloric intake necessary to support the fantastic changes in his body's stepped-up metabolism. Loew was uncoordinated and fumbled whatever he touched, another sign that he hadn't become used to the freakish growth.

Tom took a step forward and spoke. "Dr. Loew, we need to talk."

The now imposing figure of Dr. Loew whirled and flung a beaker at Tom. The unexpected attack took Tom by surprise. He flinched, but the heavy glass vessel struck him on the shoulder, spinning him around.

Tom looked up as Dr. Loew doubled his hands into bony fists, roared, and ponderously came for him.

DON'T TOUCH ME!" TOM CRIED. "YOU'LL GET
a shock!"

Loew didn't listen. He swung and barely
missed connecting with Tom's head. Tom
danced back, clumsy in the electrosuit.

"I just want to talk, Dr. Loew. You've contaminated the bay. You have to cooperate so
we can put it right."

"I don't take orders from you, little boy,"
Loew rasped out, his voice hoarse from the
hGh. "I'm the big man now!"

"Don't!" Tom couldn't avoid Loew's arm
brushing across his electrosuit. The charge
leapt from the suit to the warped scientist.

Loew screamed and staggered back, falling

140

heavily to the floor. He was stunned, but only momentarily. The rage burning in Loew's eyes told Tom he would have to use another tactic—quick. If Loew touched him again, the charge would be much less powerful. A third time would discharge the electrosuit completely, making it useless.

The crazed man slowly rose to his feet and lumbered toward him. Tom scuttled backward.

"Melanie!" Tom yelled. The name had a startling effect on Dr. Loew. The man skidded to a halt and just stared. His bloodshot eyes bulged slightly, and Tom saw a vein in his temple pounding fiercely, but he was listening.

"Melanie wants to help you, Dr. Loew," Tom said, more softly.

"Mel," the man croaked.

"She wants you to stop dumping the dangerous growth hormone into the bay," Tom said.

"Need to talk to her," Loew grated out. "Where is she?"

"Will you stop the dumping? I've begun cleaning up the damage you've done, but you mustn't throw any more hGh into Laguna Pequeña."

"Mel," Dr. Loew repeated. Muscles bulged under his too-small lab coat. If he wanted,

Tom knew, Loew could rip him apart and never notice the effort.

"She's down at the beach," Tom said. "We can meet her there. She wants to talk, but she's frightened of what you've become."

"Didn't want this to happen," Loew said. Then madness crept back into his eyes. "Melanie!"

"At the beach right here," Tom said, playing for time. "Do you know what a horrible effect your hGh dumping has had on the marine life there?"

"You, Swift, you wanted to ruin me, to keep me down because I am a dwarf ... was a dwarf ... small. Not now." Dr. Loew appeared confused.

"We can meet Melanie at the beach. It's not far. She wants to show you something."

Dr. Loew pushed past him, got another shock that simply made him jerk, and strode down the corridor. Tom followed, wondering if he was doing the right thing. The electrosuit made him even clumsier than the hormone-enhanced Dr. Loew.

By the time Tom got outside, Dr. Loew had vanished.

Tom touched the transmitter button and spoke urgently to Rick. "Get the police down to the beach near the complex. Reasoning with Loew seems a long shot, at best. I'm not sure what he's going to do, but that's where he's headed.''

"Tom, are you all right?" came Rick's worried voice.

"I'm fine, but Loew thinks Melanie will be at the beach. Stay sharp—in his condition, he's capable of anything.''

''Tom, wait for me!''

"Call Chief Montague, Rick. Now!" Tom began skinning out of the electrosuit, careful to keep from getting shocked himself. He took a deep breath, then started running. He was fast, but Loew, despite his clumsiness, had muscles no normal person could match.

When Tom reached the beach he was out of breath and Loew was nowhere in sight. Then Tom heard a loud animal-like bellow and turned in the direction from which it had come.

Some distance down the beach he saw Loew. To Tom's puzzlement, the scientist ripped off his clothing. He flailed around, battling an imaginary foe, and then sank to his knees. Tom thought the man had lost his mind completely. But as Tom drew closer he could see that the monster Loew fought was all too real. Crawling out of the surf was a creature that looked like a huge shark—with four rudimentary legs.

"Get back!" Tom shouted over the ocean's

roar. Loew gave no sign that he'd heard and remained kneeling in the sand.

Frozen with a mixture of fear and fascination, Tom could only stare as the monster opened its mouth, showing double rows of razor-sharp yellow teeth. It snapped and lunged, then crashed to the beach a few feet from the scientist.

Tom shook himself and ran hard to get to Loew. Now he could see the creature's eyes, frighteningly human. Its flesh hung in rotting gobbets from the shark's sides, pieces falling off as it struggled forward. The tiny feet thrashed away at the sand until the mutated shark rose up once more. It began to walk.

"I never meant for this to happen," Loew sobbed. "What an abomination!"

Again the shark-thing lunged and snapped viciously at Dr. Loew. It snorted foam and took another hesitant step on its stubby legs. Loew balled his fists and let out a howl of mindless rage. He rushed forward. To Tom's horror, he saw that the mutated scientist was intent on grappling with the beast.

"Dr. Loew, wait! The police will be here soon." Tom held back when he saw Loew wrestling with the walking monster. Razor-sharp teeth flashed in the afternoon sunlight, then clamped shut with prodigious power on Loew's muscle-swollen arm.

The man roared like a wounded lion and wrapped his other arm around the shark. The two, man and shark-thing, crashed into the water. Blood frothed and foamed on the tide.

"Get to land! It can't maneuver well there," Tom called, but the pair vanished underwater. He started to go to Dr. Loew's aid when he heard sirens behind him. He looked over his shoulder and saw that the police had arrived. Two officers rushed up with service revolvers drawn.

"There, help him," Tom shouted. He pointed into the water.

A small patch of bloody foam marked the place where Dr. Loew—and the shark-thing created with his growth hormone—had disappeared.

Neither surfaced.

"Call the Coast Guard," one officer said into his walkie-talkie. "We've got a shark attack near the Southside Industrial Complex." He stared at the slowly spreading blood on the water and muttered, "At least I think it was a shark."

"It was," Tom said, but the memory of the legs and the shark-thing walking out of the water caused him to shiver.

"The Coast Guard will take care of everything," the officer said. "It's all over now."

"Yes," Tom agreed, "it's all over."

*   *   *

Dan Coster's band cranked up the volume, and Tom felt the music's vibration through the sand as much as he heard it. He saw his friends dancing and enjoying themselves more than they had in the past three weeks. Then came the announcement over the PA system.

"Ladies and gentlemen," said Mayor Zamora, "the first round of the Laguna Pequeña Surfing Invitational is about to begin!"

Attention turned to the huge breakers piling up a hundred yards offshore. The first surfers caught waves and began their rides to the cheers of the crowd. The television cameras caught every instant of the competition.

Dan came up beside Tom. "This looks like our big chance, Tom-Tom. National cable, maybe a shot at doing a commercial for Super-Glide Surfboards, and I'm a surefire winner. Who'd have thought this would have gone down a few weeks back? Even that goof Carlton has crawled back into his hole."

"You just didn't have any faith in our boy genius," Rick said. "And what's this about having a lock on the competition? I don't go out for twenty minutes. *Then* you'll see winning form."

Tom shook his head. Rick didn't have that good a chance. Dozens of world-class surfers had shown up for the invitational, ensuring the meet's success.

"They ought to be publicly thanking you, Tom," Sandra said, coming over to them. "If you hadn't cleaned everything up, Laguna Pequeña would still be deserted and the invitational would never have been held."

"Yeah, that hungry bacteria gunk you sprayed out there worked like a charm," Dan said. "Even the Coast Guard marveled at how well it worked." He looked up and said, "Oops, got to go. They're calling my number."

"Go on," Rick said. "I want to watch you wipe out."

"No way, you clueless beach bum," Dan countered, grabbing his board and running into the surf.

Tom started to join them when he saw Melanie standing at the edge of the crowd. He went over to her, and they walked down the beach a bit.

"Hi, Melanie. How are you feeling?" he said.

"Hello, Tom," she said. "I'm doing just fine now, thanks to you. I wanted to see you before I left."

"Where are you going?"

"I can't stay around here, not after everything that's happened," Melanie said.

147

"No one blames you," Tom said softly.

"Maybe not," she answered, "but I need to get away. You understand, don't you?"

"Yes," Tom said. "I wish you would stay, though. You have so much to do. Loew Industries can—"

"No!" Melanie lowered her eyes. "Sorry, but I can't. I've just talked with your father. Swift Enterprises will be overseeing my dad's facilities for now. Then there'll be a court-ordered auction. And I'll see that the majority of the money goes toward pollution-prevention programs," Melanie said. She paused for a moment, then added, "I can't find the words to thank you for all you've done." She leaned forward and gave Tom a quick kiss on the cheek, and then headed for her car before he could say anything.

As he watched her drive away he heard Rick shouting to him.

"Hey, Tom! Dan made it to the second round. Come on over."

Tom ran down to the shoreline. Dan came out of the water grinning from ear to ear.

"What a ride! I've got it bagged!" Dan crowed.

"He does, Rick," Sandra said.

"He looked mighty good," Mandy chimed in.

"I'll beat you fourteen ways to Thursday, Rick!" Dan said, doing a dance in the sand.

"Uh, Tom," Rick said, "can you help me out? Dan did make a pretty ride. Can you whip up some kind of super-duper invention that will make me fly out there?"

"Make you fly? Sure, Rick—we can make you fly!" Tom exchanged a quick look with Sandra and their friends. They all rushed Rick at once, hoisted him into the air, and tossed him into the surf.

Rick came up sputtering and said, "What a time for you to regain your sense of humor! Why don't we just skip the rest of the competition and go for some pizza—huh, guys? You wouldn't want Tom's best friend to embarrass himself, would you?"

But Tom and the others were laughing too hard to say anything.

Tom's next adventure:

Tom's work on a psychotronic translator, which deciphers brain waves and reads minds, has been interrupted by a small earthquake. But the minor tremor may have major consequences: A terrorist group using stolen nuclear material has vowed to turn the epicenter of the next—and much more massive—quake into ground zero!

Determined to prevent the doomsday quake, Tom undertakes a daring journey toward the center of the earth. But deep beneath the surface, he makes a startling discovery. He must make contact with an unknown intelligence by using the psychotronic translator. And failure could mean catastrophe—as all of southern California teeters on the edge of the abyss ... in Tom Swift #12, *Death Quake*.